A Hidden Enemy

Barlow hoped these Blackfeet were more interested in counting coup than in raising hair. That notion, however, fled when an arrow suddenly appeared in the tree next to his head. He had heard nothing until the sharp thunk of the arrow landing.

"Pustulant bastards," he muttered. His eyes worriedly but categorically scanned the trees as he tried to estimate where the arrow had come from. He thought he saw a slight movement in the brush that did not seem right. He lifted his rifle and aimed, waiting as the sweat beaded on his forehead. When he thought he spotted another slight movement, he fired.

"Waugh!" he muttered in satisfaction as someone fell in the brush. He wasn't sure he had killed the enemy, but he knew he had hit him. As he reloaded by touch and experience, he kept scanning the trees and brush.

Barlow didn't know why he moved, but he dropped forward onto his face, and the Blackfoot warrior's knife blade merely slashed through the back of his shirt and left barely a scratch in his flesh . . .

DON'T MISS THESE
ALL-ACTION WESTERN SERIES
FROM THE BERKLEY PUBLISHING GROUP

THE GUNSMITH by J. R. Roberts
Clint Adams was a legend among lawmen, outlaws, and ladies.
They called him . . . the Gunsmith.

LONGARM by Tabor Evans
The popular long-running series about U.S. Deputy Marshal
Long—his life, his loves, his fight for justice.

SLOCUM by Jake Logan
Today's longest-running action Western. John Slocum rides
a deadly trail of hot blood and cold steel.

BUSHWHACKERS by B. J. Lanagan
An action-packed series by the creators of Longarm! The
rousing adventures of the most brutal gang of cutthroats ever
assembled—Quantrill's Raiders.

DIAMONDBACK by Guy Brewer
Dex Yancey is Diamondback, a southern gentleman turned
con man when his brother cheats him out of the family for-
tune. Ladies love him. Gamblers hate him. But nobody pulls
one over on Dex . . .

WILDGUN by Jack Hanson
Will Barlow's continuing search for his daughter, kidnapped
by the Blackfeet Indians who slaughtered the rest of his
family.

Wildgun
Blood Trail

Jack Hanson

JOVE BOOKS, NEW YORK

This is a work of fiction. Names, characters, places, and incidents are
either the product of the author's imagination or are used fictitiously,
and any resemblance to actual persons, living or dead, business
establishments, events, or locales is entirely coincidental.

BLOOD TRAIL

A Jove Book / published by arrangement with
the author

PRINTING HISTORY
Jove edition / July 2000

All rights reserved.
Copyright © 2000 by Penguin Putnam Inc.
This book may not be reproduced in whole or part,
by mimeograph or any other means, without permission.
For information address: The Berkley Publishing Group,
a division of Penguin Putnam Inc.,
375 Hudson Street, New York, New York 10014.

The Penguin Putnam Inc. World Wide Web site address is
http://www.penguinputnam.com

ISBN: 0-515-12870-8

A JOVE BOOK®
Jove Books are published by The Berkley Publishing Group,
a division of Penguin Putnam Inc.,
375 Hudson Street, New York, New York 10014.
JOVE and the "J" design
are trademarks belonging to Penguin Putnam Inc.

PRINTED IN THE UNITED STATES OF AMERICA

10 9 8 7 6 5 4 3 2 1

1

THE FIRST THOUGHT Will Barlow had when he opened his eyes was, *Where the hell am I?* He was in a place he found mighty familiar, but he could not for the life of him put a finger on it. He was not really worried or anxious, as the place seemed to encompass him with a warm contentment. The soft feather bed enveloped him in comfort.

Still, as secure as he felt, he needed to get up and figure things out. Things like where he was and how he had gotten here. He pushed himself up with his arms, ready to swing his legs off the side of the bed, but froze for a moment and then sank back down on the bed as fire roared through his chest.

As he closed his eyes, visions swam through his mind, mingling with agony—scenes of battle, a loyal dog pincushioned with arrows, his anger and worry, fresh pain from a Blackfoot arrow that had . . .

He sucked in deep breaths, trying to ease the pain in his chest. Then he eased his eyes open. A moment later, he spotted the dark tartan kilt hanging on a wall, and it became clear. He smiled a little.

"Duncan!" he bellowed, and immediately cursed himself for doing so, as it brought a new burst of agony to his chest.

He had managed to calm himself by the time his father-in-law entered the room.

"Well, lad," Duncan Stewart said with a smile, " 'tis time ye were awake. Aye, ye've been sleepin' for a long time."

"How'd I git here, Duncan?" Barlow asked, trying to ignore the flames in his chest.

"Ye were delivered unto us by God's gracious hand," Stewart said. "And with the aid of several Bannock Indians."

"Bannocks?" Barlow questioned.

"Aye. 'Twas a damn good thing, too, lad. Ye were close to death's door. Had it nae been for those Indians, ye would've been worm food long afore now."

"But how . . . ? Why . . . ?"

"Someone else should tell ye the rest, lad," Stewart said. "When ye think ye have the strength to sit up."

Barlow bit his lip so hard that he drew blood when he tried to rise, and the pain sliced through him like the Blackfoot arrowhead had. "Mayhap I ought to keep my damn questions to myself till I'm a bit stronger."

"Aye, tha' 'twould be best, I think, lad. I dunna how much ye could grasp of it all, anyway. Not that there's much bad in what we have to tell ye. But ye should be clear of mind to hear it."

Barlow nodded. Exhaustion was overcoming the agony, and he simply wanted to sleep, to let the bliss of the Land of Nod wash away the pain and confusion. He did not even hear his father-in-law's quiet, "Good night, lad."

•   •   •

Barlow awoke periodically over the next several days and even managed to slurp down a little fish soup. As much as he disliked it, the warm broth gave him a bit of strength, which he appreciated. Still, it was more than another week before he felt he could sit up without wincing from his pain. He was still sore and incredibly weak, which was odd to him, but he could manage that. One day he was sitting up as Stewart entered the room. "All right, Duncan," he said, "tell me."

"In a bit, lad," Stewart replied. "I'll be back in a few ticks." He was gone more than an hour and returned with White Bear in tow. The Shoshoni looked weak, drawn, tentative in his movements.

"You all right, White Bear?" Barlow asked, shocked at the Indian's condition.

"Better'n you are, old chap," White Bear growled. His voice was as deep as ever, but was nowhere near as forceful as it had been.

"Sure as hell don't seem like it, hoss," Barlow countered.

"At least I'm up and about, you bloody bugger, not lollygagging around like you are." He grinned. It was a pale imitation of his normal smile, but it relieved Barlow a little.

"Up and about my ass, boy," Barlow growled. His own voice was hardly more than a whisper. "I expect it's only Mrs. Stewart's broom handle stuck up your hindquarters keepin' you standin'."

White Bear grinned and took a seat. "That ain't true, old chap," he noted, then added, "but it sure does feel like it sometimes."

Barlow nodded, familiar with the feeling, and hating it every bit as much as he knew White Bear did. "So, ol' hoss, how'd we git here?" he asked after a few moments' silence.

"You remember the battle?" White Bear countered.

Barlow nodded. "Goddamn Blackfeet sons of bitches," he muttered hatefully. "Kilt poor ol' Buffler. Made a riddle of that ol' dog with arrows. Damn 'em. I took me an arrow in the chest, which hooked on the bone, best as I could tell. You seemed even worse than me at the time. Last I remember was gittin' your near-dead ass into a travios and headin' this way. Never expected, really, to make it, though."

"Didn't. Not on our own."

"Duncan said some Bannocks brung us in?" Barlow questioned.

"Aye." He paused. "But you did get us a good long ways, old chap. I was unconscious most of the time, but I woke up now and again and managed to piece some things together. You got us into Bannock country, somehow. I really can't say how you did."

"I cain't either," Barlow responded with a grimace.

White Bear shrugged. "Doesn't matter. Ye did git us fairly close to Bloody Hide's village. He and some of the men out hunting came across us and took us back to the village. From what I understand, Gretchen and Red Moccasins tended to us as best they could, and their medicine man did what he could. But they realized after a spell that we were in far worse shape than they could deal with. I think I heard someone say that you were babblin' on about gettin' to Fort Vancouver."

"So the Bannocks brung us here?" Barlow asked.

"Aye," Stewart said. "In the dead of the winter, too. Must've been hard travelin' for them in some parts, lad. And their arrival caused a wee little stir around here, too, I'll say, lad. Some of the lads were thinkin' that maybe the Bannocks were the ones who did ye wrong, but I ne'er heard of the Bannocks doon such a thing. Then some wanted to rub out ol' White Bear there.

Damn fools. But Dr. McLoughlin got everyone calmed down right off and while he was lookin' the two of ye o'er, he talked to the Bannocks and learned what had happened. Then he went to work on ye, too. Took him a wee long time to get that arrowhead out of ye, Will."

"Reckon it did." He paused, thinking, then asked, "The Bannocks still around?"

"Nae," Stewart responded. "They didna like the looks of some of the men, and as soon as everyone had turned their attentions to you, those Indians hurried off."

"Cain't say as I blame 'em," Barlow said with a shake of the head.

"Aye," Stewart agreed.

"How about you, White Bear?" Barlow asked. "You been treated fair whilst you been here?"

"Mostly. There's a few bloody bastards here don't look kindly on a Shoshoni. But no one's bothered me, really. I think Dr. McLoughlin has had something to do with that."

"Reckon he has," Barlow said with a nod.

"Who of the Bannocks actually brung us here, White Bear?" Barlow asked.

"Bloody Hide led the way," White Bear said, to Barlow's surprise. "Two warriors, Gretchen and Red Moccasins."

"We owe them folks our lives, hoss," Barlow said.

"I know that, old chap."

Barlow sighed as exhaustion enveloped him again. He hated being this way—so tired all the time, so weak, incapable of doing just about anything. In some ways, he just wanted to give in to it, to submit and let the world fade away. But one thought was ever present in his mind and always gave him the will to live—the thought that Anna was still out there somewhere, probably being abused in a Blackfoot camp. That had, and always would, keep him going. As he lay back down, he could see her face in his mind, and he held it there. I'm comin' Little One, he said in his thoughts. And he vowed to do whatever was necessary to regain his strength as soon as possible so he could get out on the trail to look for his daughter again.

He thought it somewhat fortunate that it was still deep in winter. That would give him at least a couple of months to recover. He felt he should be ready to ride out again as soon as spring arrived.

Barlow began to doubt that over the next week or so. He was angry—furious—at his lack of strength and the inability to do little more than the most minor things. His mind raged against the once big, powerful body that had always sustained him but was now a dismal disappointment.

White Bear was recovering well, and while Barlow could not see his own rehabilitation, the Shoshoni could see it. As could Stewart. Each day Barlow grew minutely stronger, ate a little more, moved a little more, showed less and less of the wear that the wound had inflicted on him.

Within another week and a half, Barlow was up and about, moving tentatively, but moving. In a few more days he was able to care for himself for the most part, which alleviated much of his consternation. He was repulsed by the thought of someone having to help him with his most personal needs. Now that he could take care of those on his own, he felt considerably better about himself, and it seemed to be a breakthrough, pushing him to more improvement.

Hampering his recovery somewhat was his deep sense of loss at Buffalo's death. Not only was Barlow stuck—again—with being unable to find Anna, his beloved dog was gone, too. He had never realized until now just how much he cared for the big, shaggy Newfoundland. The dog had been loyal, intelligent, courageous, a good traveling companion, and the best alarm for when enemies were lurking about. Barlow was not sure how he was going to be able to take to the field on his quest again without his devoted dog.

Barlow never said anything about missing the dog, but those close to him—mostly White Bear and Duncan Stewart—could see it in his face and movements. Finally, White Bear said to Stewart, "We've got to do something for the old chap."

"Aye," Stewart agreed. "But what can we do?"

"Find him another bloody dog," White Bear snapped. "I can't bear to see Will like this, and I'll be damned if I'm gonna travel with him when he's bloody melancholy."

Stewart grinned. He knew that the Shoshoni cared more for Barlow than he was letting on and was speaking so gruffly to hide his affection for the former mountain man. "Aye," he agreed, " 'twould be a good thing. I'll ask aroond."

Barlow sat on his bed in the Stewart home, stretching and relaxing his chest muscles, ignoring the pain. It was now bearable, and he was determined to rebuild his strength as quickly as possible. He continued doing his exercise when White Bear walked into the room, but then he stopped and looked at White Bear in bewilderment. "What the hell are you grinnin' at, hoss?" he asked, annoyed as well as puzzled.

"Got something for you, old chap," the Shoshoni said, his grin threatening to split his face in two. He stepped aside, out of the doorway.

Stewart backed into the room sweating and cursing as he heaved on something. Finally the seemingly dead weight at the end of the rope he held was also in the room. Stewart straightened, gasping for breath. "For you," he panted.

Barlow could not believe his eyes. "Where . . . what . . . how . . . who?" He rose slowly and walked to the dog. It was another Newfoundland, and it looked like an exact, though younger and slightly smaller, version of Buffalo. He knelt in front of the dog, which was skittish and worried, and kept jerking at the rope Stewart had tied around his neck. "Where'd you get him?" Barlow asked in a hushed, almost reverent voice.

"Some old trapper had him," Stewart said. "And was nae treatin' him well, I can tell ye."

"No wonder he's so spooked," Barlow agreed. He reached a hand out, palm up, toward the dog, which growled a little. "Don't you worry none, dog," he said quietly, "ain't no one here gonna hurt you."

"We figure he's maybe two years old, old chap," White Bear said. "At least from what we could tell from Fleming, the bloody bastard who had him."

"He's beautiful," Barlow said, still looking at the dog. He tried again to bring his hand to the animal, and this time managed. He gently rubbed the fur on the animal's throat. The Newfoundland decided he liked that and relaxed a little.

"How much did he cost you boys?" Barlow asked, finally looking up at his two friends. "I'll pay you back soon's I can."

"He's a gift, ye damned fool," Stewart snapped. He was still a little annoyed at the exercise he had gotten trying to practically drag the dog here.

"Well, I hope you didn't pay too much for him." He squirmed forward, close to the dog, which didn't shy away.

"Weren't much," White Bear said. "But more than Fleming deserved."

"Oh?" Barlow asked, looking up again, this time in surprise.

"Aye," Stewart said with a grin. "Our Shoshoni friend here was of the mind that we should just go and take the dog from Fleming, and perhaps pay him with a bullet to the head for his maltreatment of the animal."

"Damn right," White Bear agreed. "That bloody bugger didn't deserve a tuppence."

"Ye're probably right, White Bear," Stewart said. He grinned a little. He would have agreed to White Bear's idea—and in principle he did—but he figured that paying in cash instead of just killing the man would be far more palatable to the officers at Fort Vancouver. Not that anyone would care what happened to Georgie Fleming, but he could see no reason to raise any kind of stink at all if it wasn't necessary.

"So, what will ye name the new beastie?" Stewart asked after a short silence.

Still awestruck, Barlow managed to smile. "Well, Duncan, you know my penchant for naming whatever mount I'm usin' for ridin' Beelzebub, after the original." When Stewart nodded, Barlow said, "Well, I reckon that can work jist as well with dogs. My friends, meet the new Buffler—Buffler 2."

"He's gonna take some workin', old chap," White Bear said with a wide grin.

"Reckon he will. But he'll be worth it. You wait and see."

2

IT TOOK A considerable amount of work, but the dog began responding slowly but surely. Not that Barlow did that much actual training. He simply treated the Newfoundland well, gave it lots of attention, and firmly but patiently showed it what he wanted it to do. Buffalo 2 blossomed under the care and attention, and was eager to please his new master.

The Newfoundland also helped Barlow flourish. Within days of getting the young dog, Barlow was showing strong signs of physical recovery. Soon afterward, he surpassed White Bear in his rehabilitation, much to the Shoshoni's annoyance. But soon they both had regained most of their strength and vigor. Barlow, who had lost nearly fifty pounds, began eating prodigiously and soon regained his lost muscle. As part of their rehabilitation, Barlow and White Bear wrestled in friendly competition and began spending more time in the woods near Fort Vancouver, restoring their hunting and tracking skills.

By late March, they were pretty much their old selves,

but then frustration set in. Barlow, especially, wanted to get on the trail. As a former mountain man, he had no liking for the Blackfeet to begin with. Since those Indians had taken his daughter, his hate for them had grown considerably. And he was filled with horror at what his daughter might be enduring at their hands.

Still, he could not yet leave. While the winter in the vicinity of Fort Vancouver was relatively mild, out in the mountains and on the plains where the Blackfeet made their homes, winter would still have an iron, deadly grip on the land. So Barlow chafed at the delay. Caring for the dog was only so much of a distraction, and the long hours of boredom and inactivity ate at him.

As the weeks passed, Barlow grew more and more itchy to get on the move. He growled and grumped around, annoying everyone but Buffalo, until Stewart finally griped back at him just after supper at the Stewart table one night. "Goddammit, Will," he snapped, stopping Barlow will a forkful of mutton halfway to his mouth. "Ye've complained enough, lad. Ye canna leave here just yet. We all know that. But your whining does nae make it better for anyone. 'Twill be the time to go soon enough."

"Hell, I know that, Duncan," Barlow growled. "But all this time of not bein' able to find my chil' is wearin' on me."

"No one knows that better than I do, son," Stewart said. "She is my grandbaby, after all. But your vocal vexations dunna help anything at all."

Barlow nodded, his anger rising, but knowing that his father-in-law was right. He had to calm himself, at least outwardly. "Reckon you're speakin' true, Duncan," he said quietly. He sat in thought for a while, then said, "I'll be leavin' in three weeks."

"I'll be ready," White Bear said.

"Ain't necessary, hoss," Barlow said. "You're free to head back toward your home any time you want. The search for Anna ain't really your concern."

"Like hell, old chap," White Bear protested. "Because I was made a fool of, Anna was taken and given to those damn Blackfeet. That bloody well makes it my concern. And if that weren't enough, then bein' damn near killed by those bloody Blackfeet certainly makes it my concern. I fully intend, old chap, to ride out with you when the time comes and bloody well stick with you, my dear chap, until we find Anna."

"You're certain about that, are you, hoss?" Barlow asked with some heat. He liked White Bear considerably, but he wasn't sure he wanted the Shoshoni with him. He did not want to have the responsibility, as he saw it, for White Bear's health and safety. He had almost gotten the Shoshoni killed in the last fight with the Blackfeet; he did not want the next melee to have an even worse outcome.

Almost as if White Bear could read Barlow's mind, he said, "As a Shoshoni warrior, I have no fear of dying in battle, old chap. That I came close a few months ago means nothing. No more than it does to you. If I go under at the hands of the bloody Blackfeet, I will have died in glory. The only thing I ask is that you try to prevent those nasty buggers from takin' my hair."

Barlow almost grinned. "I reckon I can do that, hoss," he said dryly, "as long as I ain't havin' any trouble keepin' my own."

"Fair enough, old chap."

There was silence as the men ate until White Bear said, "My bein' with you, mate, will make it easier for you to find Anna."

"I think he's right, lad," Stewart added.

"All right, boys," Barlow growled, though he grinned

a little, "I already said he could come with me if he was damn fool enough to want to do such a thing. You got to be one of the dumbest red devils ever lived. Here you got a chance to git back to your family and your people, and you go'n choose to ride all over God's creation lookin' to raise hair on some goddamn Blackfeet."

White Bear grinned. "Somebody's got to watch over you, old chap. A lone white-eyes out there in the wilderness wouldn't have a chance against the bloody Blackfeet."

Barlow snorted, and Stewart laughed. Then Barlow chuckled. The banter had served to alleviate, even if only fractionally, the irritation that had built up by being confined to Stewart's house and environs.

"You'll be ready to move out in three weeks, hoss?" Barlow asked the Shoshoni.

"Aye," White Bear said firmly. "Every bit as much as you."

Barlow and White Bear spent the next three weeks testing themselves to make sure they were truly ready for the trail, picking up supplies a little at a time, checking out mules and horses to use for packing, and trying not to think of their quest too much, lest the exasperation at not being on the move start again.

Finally they were ready, though, and they rode through the mist and chill from Stewart's house to the fort. There they loaded several pack animals. As soon as that was done, Barlow, White Bear, and Buffalo, escorted by Stewart, headed for the ferry. They spent little time on farewells. Barlow and Stewart had been through this too many times before, and the former mountain man was eager to be on his way.

The mist was rising a little, but giving way to the omnipresent drizzle as the two men and the big dog

clacked off the ferry on the south side of the mighty
Columbia River. They swung east and moved up the
river, disappearing into the grayness within minutes.

Barlow shoved his hat a little lower against the wind
and the rain. He had always hated the rain here in the
Oregon country. It never seemed to stop. It didn't often
rain hard, but it was constant, annoying. Well, not constant, he knew, though it usually seemed that way. Even
when the drizzle wasn't actually falling, the air was thick
with mist and fog, making it seem like rain was still in
the air. And it was almost impossible to acknowledge
those rare times when the air actually seemed dry for a
few hours. He would be glad when they reached the
other side of the Cascade Mountains and hit the desert.
That, too, held its annoyances, but he and White Bear
would be across it before the relief at being out of the
rain faded.

Several hours later, they stopped to give the horses
and mules a breather. "Reckon I'll go make meat once
we're travelin' again," Barlow said, as he and White
Bear rested, backs against tree trunks. Buffalo 2 roamed
around, sniffing at the trees and brush and, as often as
not, leaving his ammonia-tainted mark on them. He was
enjoying his freedom, but he seemed to understand that
he should not stray too far from Barlow.

"Maybe I should do the huntin' for a spell," White
Bear said.

"What fer?" Barlow demanded more harshly than he
had meant to. He was still frustrated by his overall lack
of success in finding Anna, the rain, the slowness of their
pace, and damn near everything else.

"You remember what happened last time you went to
make meat out here," White Bear responded evenly.

Barlow gritted his teeth. It was another reason to hate
the rain and dampness and mist that constantly covered

this land. It was damn near impossible sometimes to keep powder dry, making rifles misfire too often. Finally, he sucked in a deep breath and nodded. He knew he could not continue to keep this sour humor. Not without it causing problems. "Reckon you're right, hoss," he said. Then he grinned, "But don't you dare come back with no goddamn, stinkin' fish, you hear me, you Godless savage you."

White Bear laughed. "I'd as soon put an arrow in my own bloody foot than eat fish," he said around the chuckles, "and you damn well know it, old chap."

"Jist makin' certain you hadn't changed your ways after all that salmon Mrs. Stewart foisted on us," Barlow replied, joining in his friend's laughter.

"She's a dear woman, Will, but I swear, if she'd served that damn fish one more time, I was gonna raise hair on her." He slapped his knee as the guffaws spread.

"Now that would've been something to see," Barlow sputtered through the laughter. "You chasin' after that plump ol' gal, scalpin' knife in hand, howlin' your war cry whilst Duncan was tryin' to get his damp powder to work to make wolf bait of you!"

"Does create one hell of a bloody picture, doesn't it, old chap?"

"That it does. Of course, she might've jist stood her ground against you, though. I can see it now—you with your war club and scalpin' knife, ol' Mrs. Stewart with her big ol' skillet in one hand and a goddamn stinkin' salmon in the other, jist darin' you to come agin her!"

The two roared with gales of laughter for some minutes. A few yards away, Buffalo looked at them, seemingly worried.

Finally the jollity faded, and the men rose. They tightened saddles and packs and rode off. Barlow kept to the trail roughly following the river, towing all but one of the pack animals. Buffalo trotted out in front, nose constantly sniffing, tail wagging joyfully the whole time. White Bear swung off toward the southeast, riding his pony and trailing one of the two extra mules they had.

They met again two hours later a few miles up the trail. White Bear was waiting, honing his knife as he sat against a rock when Barlow rode up. "You done good, hoss," Barlow said, noting the deer carcass across the extra mule.

"I'm so bloody thankful you think so, old chap," White Bear responded with a wide grin.

"Jist git mounted up and movin', hoss," Barlow countered with a smile. "We got us a heap of distance to cover yet before you can rest that fat, lazy carcass of yours."

"Lazy, I might give you. But fat? Not bloody well likely. Not when compared with you." Still grinning, the Shoshoni slid his knife and honing stone away, rose, and leaped onto his pony in one swift, smooth move.

The journey soon took on a decidedly monotonous tone, which they had expected. Still, the lack of anything to really focus on except the object of their quest wore on Barlow's mind. All he could do was chafe at the slowness of their travel, at the time it would take to get to Blackfoot country, and at the seemingly endless searching they would likely have to do when they got there. It all ate at Barlow, making him frequently cantankerous and surly. White Bear would usually leave Barlow alone to stew in his own biliousness during most of the day, but he seemed to have a knack of bringing his friend out of his disagreeable humor with relative ease and speed.

Though he never said anything about it, Barlow appreciated what White Bear did in these instances, and he was glad he had accepted the Shoshoni's companionship on the journey. Not only would the trek be all that more unbearable without White Bear, Barlow also knew he would need the warrior's help once they found Anna.

"You plannin' to head straight for the Blackfeet country?" White Bear asked one night.

"Yep. Why?" He thought the question foolish.

"You know, old chap, the Bannocks ain't all that far off the bloody trail for us."

"So?" Barlow sighed. He knew he was in another hostile mood, and he didn't like being that way, though it seemed there was little he could do about it.

"So," White Bear said slowly, "those people were the ones who saved our hides for us."

"I know that. But . . ."

"Don't you think it'd be bloody well proper to pay them a visit and thank them for what they did, old chap?"

"Hell, we ain't got time for such doin's. We can visit 'em later, after we . . ." A vision of Red Moccasins invaded his mind, stopping him. He could see her smooth, firm breasts, the comforting swell of her belly, and the glistening treasure that lay just below. His breath quickened at the remembrance of how it felt being inside her.

White Bear smiled as the emotions flickered across Barlow's face.

"I reckon you're right, hoss," Barlow finally said. "It ain't really out of our way. And we'll have to spend a night someplace when we're out there. Might's well be with some friendly critters."

"Friendly, yes," White Bear said with a wide grin.

"You've jist got stiff britches to have another go at Gretchen," Barlow said with a laugh, his mood lightening.

"I notice you went cross-eyed a moment ago," White Bear countered. "I don't reckon that had anything to do with a certain lass named Red Moccasins, does it?"

"Could be that it does," Barlow allowed with a laugh.

3

THEY FOLLOWED THE Columbia River for a couple more weeks, until it made its huge oxbow turn, where they picked up the Snake River. They moved as fast as they could, making better progress once they were out on the flats and in the desert, where it was still cool enough that neither men nor animals suffered. Without the almost-constant rain, or the occasional sleet or snow, travelers could made good time.

Another week on, they shifted toward the banks of the Salmon River and followed it eastward, back into the mountains, where the cold gripped them, and the ice and snow that remained made footing slick and treacherous. They slowed their pace, griping more often, but pressing on as best as they could.

They spotted several Bannock villages before they found the one they were seeking. It was just less than a month since they had left Fort Vancouver.

Barlow and White Bear were welcomed into the village with great joy. As soon as they were spotted, plans were made for a large feast and celebration, neither of which the two travelers minded. The first thing they did was to go and greet Bloody Hide, the civil chief of the band, who seemed quite happy to see them.

Suddenly, however, a look of horror crossed Bloody Hide's face. His face blanching some, he pointed in consternation at Buffalo.

Confused, Barlow asked, "What's wrong, Bloody Hide?"

"The dog. He has come back from the Land Beyond," Bloody Hide whispered.

It took a moment for realization to hit Barlow, and he grinned. "It's all right, Bloody Hide," he said, trying not to laugh out loud at the Bannock's fright. "This ain't the same dog. It's one looks jist like him. The original Buffler was put under by the goddamn Blackfeet. I got this here fella at Fort Vancouver, through the good wishes of White Bear here. This one I call Buffler 2. He's a bit smaller and younger'n the first one."

Bloody Hide relaxed a little and knelt in front of the dog, staring at the animal. The Newfoundland cocked its head quizzically and whined a little, then backed a few feet away, growling softly.

Bloody Hide smiled and rose. "It is good," he said firmly. "Different dog."

Barlow patted the big Newfoundland's head, scratching between his ears. "Yep, different," he agreed.

The two visitors left Bloody Hide, looking for the women they wanted to see. Both were waiting, shyly eager, near a couple of lodges toward one side of the camp. Leaving their horses and mules where they were, the men retired into the tipis with the women. A confused Buffalo 2 followed Barlow into the one lodge and ran around, sniffing at everything. Barlow was glad that the dog did not mark anything in there.

"Go lay down, Buffler," Barlow commanded. "Go

on." As the dog circled a few times and then plopped down heavily, Barlow turned toward Red Moccasins and pulled her close to him. "You're a sight for sore eyes, gal," he said huskily.

The woman was a beautiful, friendly, fun-loving widow of about nineteen. Barlow had found out before, when visiting this village, that she was experienced and quite lusty.

After kissing her hard, Barlow took half a step back. With a smile, Red Moccasins dropped her dress and kicked off her moccasins. Barlow watched the action with delight, and he liked what he saw. Red Moccasins was fairly tall and slender, though she had wide womanly hips, long legs, and small, upturned breasts topped by thick, very dark nipples and areolae. Her black hair was shiny with grease and hung loosely down her back. Her full lips were parted in a sensual smile, and her deep-set, dark eyes sparkled with excitement and life.

"Well?" Red Moccasins said, licking her lips a little.

"Reckon I am a mite overdressed for the occasion, ain't I?" Barlow said with a grin. He began peeling off weapons and clothes. In minutes he was as naked as she and had pulled her close to him again.

Their mouths met and hungrily ravaged each other, their tongues swirling furiously, as if unable to get enough of one another. Red Moccasins wrapped her arms around his bullish neck, and she arched her back, pushing her midsection into his rapidly stiffening manhood. He groaned around the woman's mouth, as fire burned up from his lance and heated his entire body, setting his mind aflame.

Barlow moved a big hand down and gripped a small, firm buttock. He followed with the other. Her wetness was already soaking his thigh.

Without moving her lips from his, Red Moccasins

suddenly jumped up and wrapped her lean legs around
Barlow's thick waist. His big hands on her buttocks easily helped her up. For a moment he worried, wondering
if his strength had really come fully back after being so
seriously wounded. But she was as light as a feather.

Pulling her head back, Red Moccasins smiled broadly,
her teeth gleaming white against her dark skin. She took
one arm from around Barlow's neck, not worried that
he couldn't hold her up. She reached down, took his
hardness firmly in hand, and guided him into her.

"Ahhhhh," she moaned. "I like."

"I like, too," Barlow agreed.

She slid her hand around Barlow's neck again and
pulled his head toward hers. Then her mouth devoured
his, while at the same time her hips began gyrating and
sliding on his shaft. She kept up a smooth motion that
rose and fell as well as rotated. She could feel him getting close, but she refused to speed her movements. His
breath came harshly in through his nose, as her lips were
still plastered against his. He moaned into her soft, sweet
mouth.

Red Moccasins felt her own climax rushing up on her,
and she finally quickened her hip action, ramming herself up and down on his powerful shaft. She screamed
into his mouth, as a huge shudder racked her slim body.
Her head jerked back, giving voice to her shriek of ecstasy.

"Don't stop," Barlow muttered urgently.

Red Moccasins grinned at him, lust still filling her
eyes, and she pounded away on him some more.

Barlow thought his knees would give way as he filled
her with his boiling maleness, and he worried that he
might crumple from the power of it. But though he grew
weak for some moments, he remained tall and strong,
though his face was a rictus of passion, and the veins in

his neck throbbed and bulged as his head reared back.

Red Moccasins clung to him for another minute or two, waiting until she knew he had spent all he could in her. Then she weakly slid her legs down from his hips. She stood like a newborn foal on trembling limbs, keeping her arms around his neck lest she fall. "Good!" she said breathlessly.

Barlow nodded, unsure about his ability to speak at the moment.

They stood, holding each other, trying to recover their breath, weak and dizzy from the passion but loving where they were. Finally, though, Red Moccasins took a step back. Taking one of his hands, she said, "Come. We rest."

"Good idea," Barlow gasped. They lurched toward the bed of buffalo robes and sank down. Barlow lay back, gently stroking Red Moccasins's hair and back as she sat cross-legged and straight-backed until Barlow grabbed a shank of her hair and gently tugged.

Red Moccasins smiled over her shoulder and then stretched out on her side next to him, cuddling up as close as she could. She murmured in satisfaction and contentment.

Barlow glanced at Buffalo. The dog looked puzzled and perhaps a little afraid. Barlow had wondered how the dog would react to such a thing, since he had not encountered it before. He seemed to be doing fine, if perhaps a little baffled. "Best git used to such doin's, boy," he said softly, grinning.

The Newfoundland rose warily and tentatively moved toward Barlow. The big man smiled and stretched out a hand. Buffalo 2 came close enough to be petted. Then he lay down, his side up against Barlow, who moments later fell asleep.

The pulsating of drums woke him. Barlow sat up,

wondering where Red Moccasins had gone off to. He figured she was out helping in the preparations for that night's feast and celebration. Buffalo was lying nearby, watching him. Barlow smiled at the dog, rose, and began pulling his clothes on. He was almost done when Red Moccasins entered the lodge.

"You rest good?" she asked.

Barlow nodded.

"Hungry?"

"As much as a griz after a long winter," Barlow responded with a smile.

"Things almost ready. Come."

Bannocks were beginning to gather around a central fire. The drums were still beating steadily, though the singing and dancing had not yet begun. Barlow and White Bear sat on either side of Bloody Hide. Buffalo stretched out in front of Barlow, watching the goings-on intently.

Giggling, Red Moccasins and Gretchen went off to help the other women. They all soon began serving food to the men—antelope stews, fresh cuts of roasted buffalo tongue, hump and ribs, spicy boudins. A few small bottles of whiskey began making the rounds among the men. When he took his full swigs, Barlow hoped there were not many more men in the village. Dealing with a bunch of drunken Bannocks was not something he wanted to face. But it seemed as if those were the only bottles, and when they were empty—which took only moments once each man had his share—no more appeared.

Barlow ate as he always did—prodigiously, and with gusto, though he knew when he had had his fill. Unlike the Bannocks, he could see no point of eating until he got sick, purging himself and then going back for more. He had seen that among many tribes, and it always repulsed him. Of course, he had seen many a white man do the same thing when among the Indians, and he did not like it when they did it either.

Soon after the food was served, the dancing began. First the women performed a social dance, their bodies shuffling to the pulse of the drums and the high pitched tones of flutes and eagle-bone whistles. Then some of the men performed, strutting proudly for the audience, showing off their finery. Finally, men and women began dancing together.

Red Moccasins, who had come to sit next to Barlow when the women had finished dancing, now urged her man to get up and dance with her. But the big man refused.

"I done that last time with you," he protested, "and all you got out of such doin's was sore feet where this ol' clumsy ox stomped all over you. You want to dance so bad, you can do so with someone else. I won't mind." Silently, he added, *too much*. He hoped she understood that. She seemed to have a slightly better grasp of English now than she had back in the fall, but he wasn't sure how much of it she really got.

"I stay," she said firmly, taking his huge arm in her two and squeezing hard.

"I like," he said, grinning.

After a few more dances, the men began regaling the audience with tales of their daring and courage. Barlow and White Bear were encouraged to join in, which they did, seeing as how they were no less proud of their achievements and bravery than the Bannocks. Not knowing the language, the two visitors told their tales using signs. Both were well-enough versed in using signs to keep their audience enthralled, eliciting a considerable number of whoops of approbation. And, as the Bannocks surely did, Barlow and White Bear expanded on their exploits, making themselves fighters and hunters of heroic proportions.

Dancing began again after the telling of tales, and a beaming Barlow took his seat next to Red Moccasins, who smiled widely in pride at him. She squeezed his right arm again. And, within a few minutes, whispered to him. "We go now."

"To the lodge?" he asked eagerly.

Red Moccasins nodded, smiling brightly in anticipation.

Barlow's grin widened, and he rose, pulling her up with him. Next to him, Bloody Hide was nearly asleep and unaware of their leaving. Out of the circle of firelight, Barlow scooped Red Moccasins up and carried her to the lodge and then inside. He placed her down on the bed of robes, ignoring Red Moccasins's sister and brother-in-law, who were making love nearby. "Go on lay down, boy," Barlow commanded Buffalo. The dog did so, though he didn't appear to like it. He looked as if he wanted to go explore what the other couple was doing.

As Barlow hurriedly stripped, Red Moccasins squiggled out of her dress and moccasins, all the while avidly watching Barlow. She lay back, hands clasped behind her head, and watched as Barlow knelt before her. She was open for him, wanting him.

Barlow stretched out between her legs and flicked his tongue against her womanhood. She was sopping already. He tongued and licked at her femininity, and in seconds Red Moccasins was moaning. Her hips and buttocks writhed. Having trouble keeping aim at his target, since she was wriggling so fiercely, Barlow grabbed the woman's round, firm buttocks in his hands, which gave him more control. He buried his face in her wetness and devoured her womanhood as is he were starving and this was the only sustenance on earth.

Red Moccasins yelped and moaned, bucked and squiggled. Her passionate groans drowned out the sounds of lovemaking from across the lodge. Suddenly she grabbed Barlow's hair and smashed his face down onto her cushiony secret place, and ground it up against his face. She released a high-pitched shriek and seemed to freeze in position for some moments before her body relaxed and she sank back onto the buffalo robes.

Barlow lifted his wet face and grinned hugely. Then he moved up between her legs. Though she had not caught her breath yet, Red Moccasins eagerly grabbed his stiff shaft and guided him into her soaking, needy tunnel. As he plunged into her to the root, she wrapped her arms around his back, clawing at him with her short, ragged nails and sliding her legs up over the backs of his legs.

About ready to burst, Barlow rode her hard and fast, punching in and out of her velvet sheath. And in only moments, he was roaring like a rutting bull buffalo. He tensed and his muscles bunched as he spilled his hot seed into her.

Utterly spent, he fell on her and barely managed to roll himself over and off of her so he didn't smother her with his bulk and weight. He was way behind on his breathing.

4

BARLOW AND WHITE Bear pulled out of the Bannock village the next morning but not nearly as early as they had planned. In fact, it was approaching midmorning by the time the white man mounted his big mule, Beelzebub, and the Shoshoni swung onto his pony. Neither man said much as they clopped slowly out of the camp, but each had a smile plastered on his face that bespoke of the morning's activities.

Barlow and Red Moccasins had made love happily and with great abandon, blissfully ignoring the other people in the lodge and the dog, who finally pushed his way out the flap of the tipi, seemingly with a disgusted air about him.

The two lovers had laughed at that, and then went back to their pleasuring.

Soon afterward, Barlow dressed and strolled outside to look for White Bear, but when he neared the lodge the Shoshoni was sharing with Gretchen—and others— he heard the unmistakable sounds of them enjoying carnal pleasures. He grinned and walked on, stopping at

Bloody Hides's lodge, where he ate. Then, as he sat listening to the civil chief's monotone, Barlow felt a renewed desire for Red Moccasins. He made a polite farewell and headed back to the lodge. There he found Red Moccasins waiting for him and more than willing to have an enjoyable time with him again.

When they were done, rested, and dressed, they headed outside. Blue Hawk, one of Red Moccasins's brothers-in-law, greeted them and said in Bannock, "Your friend, the Shoshoni, was looking for you a little while ago." He grinned widely.

Red Moccasins translated as best she could for Barlow, who suddenly laughed. He explained what had happened when he had gone to White Bear's lodge not long ago.

Laughing, Barlow and Red Moccasins headed for White Bear's lodge again, but once more, they learned that the Shoshoni and Gretchen were quite occupied. "Again?" Red Moccasins asked.

Barlow grinned. "Again," he responded, enthusiastically. They headed back to their lodge.

Finally it had to end. And just as Barlow and Red Moccasins were finishing another round, White Bear came calling.

Red Moccasins told the Shoshoni and Gretchen to come in, and they joined Barlow at the small fire in the lodge. Red Moccasins served them all some coffee and meat. Then she sat, too.

"Couldn't keep up with me again, eh, hoss?" Barlow said, grinning.

"We started earlier," White Bear countered. "And did it longer and more often."

"Like hell," Barlow said with a laugh. "Mayhap we should ask Gretchen to tell the whole truth of these doins."

"You wouldn't like the truth," White Bear said, trying to hold back his own laughter.

"That woman'd lie through her teeth for you, hoss," Barlow said with a chuckle.

"Oh, and Red Moccasins wouldn't, old chap?"

"I reckon she would." Barlow grinned at the Bannock woman, who smiled back confidently.

"You near ready to ride, old chap?" White Bear asked as he shoveled food into his mouth.

Barlow nodded. "Soon's I finish fillin' my meatbag and git our plunder packed."

"And . . . again?" Red Moccasins hinted with powerful eagerness.

"Again . . . maybe," Barlow said with a laugh. "You nearabout wore me out already, woman." He glanced askance at White Bear, and added, "And don't you go sayin' nothin' either, hoss. You looked like you been drug around the prairie by a herd of goddamn buffler."

White Bear laughed. "I bloody well feel that way, too, old chap. These women sure have a way of sappin' a man."

"That they do," Barlow agreed.

The two men finished eating and headed out toward their horses and mules. Within an hour, they were riding out of the village, after having said a respectful good-bye to Bloody Hide and an enthusiastic, if considerably brief, farewell to Red Moccasins and Gretchen.

Their joviality faded fast as soon as they cleared the last lodges of the small village. With a suddenness that would have been startling to anyone who had seen it, their attention shifted in the blink of an eye from pleasure-loving rogues to hard-eyed, focused hunters.

They pushed hard that day since they had gotten such a late start. In their revised frame of mind, they were angry now at having wasted so much time this morning, despite the pleasures that it had brought. So they kept a punishing pace, riding until well after dark before making a cold camp. They turned in after a poor meal of jerky and water.

As usual, Barlow awoke first. He considered not building a fire but then decided that they should have a decent morning meal, for it would be another long day on the trail. He gathered up kindling and a bit of wood and then pulled out his fire-making kit. A few quick clacks of steel against flint, and the tinder caught. He nursed it to life and then set it amid the kindling. Once that caught, he added some bigger sticks and then went to fill their small coffeepot with water. Smashing some beans against a rock, he poured them into the water and set the pot near the growing flames. By the time he had hung some strips of almost-fresh meat brought from the village over the fire on sticks, White Bear was awake.

While they waited for the meat and coffee, the two men began loading the supplies on the pack animals. They ate swiftly and then finished packing and saddling their horses. White Bear kicked dirt over the fire, and the two men pulled themselves onto their riding animals. "C'mon, Buffler," Barlow called to the dog. "Time to go."

They rode out with the big Newfoundland bounding all around. Though he still missed the original, Barlow was glad he had the new Buffalo along with him. The animal was turning into a fine companion.

By the second day, they were riding cautiously since Bloody Hide's village was not far from the edge of Blackfoot country. Barlow didn't understand why Bloody Hide would allow his village to sit so near to the territory to the Bannocks' enemies, but he suspected it was a show of courage by the civil chief and his band. Barlow also suspected that part of the reason Bloody

Hide allowed it was because the Blackfeet were not nearly as powerful as they had been some years ago.

They headed southeast from the Salmon River, traveling for two days before encountering the Lemhi River and turning eastward. They moved into Lemhi Pass, and when the came out on the other side, they were in what could be considered Blackfoot territory deep in the Bitterroot Range.

Three days after coming down out of the pass, the two men were making a small camp in the late afternoon when Buffalo 2 suddenly stopped roaming around and stood. His head perked up and a low growl eased up out of his big throat.

Barlow froze with a pack while unloading a mule and glanced at the dog. White Bear was off a ways in the trees, collecting firewood. Barlow began scanning the area around him and let his nose and ears investigate the air. He quietly set the pack down on the ground and picked up his rifle. He faded back behind some brush, still trying to figure out what was bothering the Newfoundland. The dog's ears flattened, and the growling became more fierce, more urgent.

Barlow snapped his fingers twice, rapidly. Buffalo 2 cocked his head, growled once more in the original direction, then darted off toward Barlow. He stopped next to his master and stood, growling softly again. Barlow knelt and patted the back of the dog's thick neck. "What's out there, Buffler?" he asked quietly. "Blackfeet? Where are they?"

He hoped that the dog would indicate where the enemy—if that's what it was—was with the way he acted, but Buffalo seemed to be trying to pick up sounds from several directions. He was still growling intermittently.

"Hush, dog," Barlow commanded in a whisper.

The dog stopped growling, but kept cocking his head

this way and that, indicating that there was still someone out there. Barlow could hear nothing but the sighing of the wind in the trees and some magpies and stellar jays screeching out their raucous tunes.

But at least one of the sounds didn't seem right to Barlow, and he knew something was wrong. The bird call was too deep-throated, as best he knew. He stayed on one knee next to Buffalo, knowing now that an attack was imminent. The trouble was, he had no idea of where it would come from or when. Nor did he know how many enemies were out there.

He hoped these Blackfeet were more interested in counting coup than in raising hair. That notion, however, fled when an arrow suddenly appeard in the tree next to his head. He had heard nothing until the sharp thunk of the arrow landing.

"Pustulant bastards," he muttered. His eyes worriedly but categorically scanned the trees as he tried to estimate where the arrow had come from. He thought he saw a slight movement in the brush that did not seem right. He lifted his rifle and aimed, waiting as the sweat beaded on his forehead. When he thought he spotted another slight movement, he fired.

"Waugh!" he muttered in satisfaction as someone fell in the brush. He wasn't sure he had killed the enemy, but he knew he had hit him. As he reloaded by touch and experience, he kept scanning the trees and brush.

Buffalo had quieted down some, though he remained as alert as ever, his ears twitching toward the sounds only he could hear. He suddenly squatted and his ears lowered, as he pitched his head toward his right. Then he backed off some, moving a few feet away. Barlow looked at him, wondering where the attack that seemed imminent would come from.

Barlow didn't know why he moved, but he dropped

forward onto his face, and a Blackfoot warrior's knife blade merely slashed through the back of his shirt and left barely a scratch in his flesh.

The warrior reared back for another plunge of the knife, but two hundred pounds of black fury knocked him moccasins over tea kettle. The Newfoundland backed off then, almost lying on his belly, growling and snarling, but uncertain of what to do next.

"Git him, Buffler," Barlow said evenly, pushing himself over and partially up. "Go on, git him."

The dog shot forward, like a great black arrow, uncertainty gone, and in a moment had the Blackfoot on the ground and was tearing chunks of flesh off the frantically battling warrior.

White Bear slipped silently up next to Barlow, startling him when he whispered, "I counted four ponies."

"Goddammit, hoss, don't sneak up on me like that. Christ, you like to give me the apoplexy like that."

White Bear shrugged. "Sorry, old chap." He glanced at Buffalo 2. "Looks like that dog's evened the odds a wee bit."

Barlow nodded. "And I put a lead pill in one a bit ago. Ain't sure if he went under or if I just wounded him."

"Then there's still two, maybe three of the bloody buggers out there."

"And damned well hid, too." Barlow sighed. "Where'd you spot them ponies?"

White Bear pointed.

Barlow nodded, though he could see nothing. At least now he had a general idea of where the Blackfeet would eventually go. "Reckon I ought to go see if that one I shot is gone under or not," he finally said.

"Watch your hair, old chap."

"You, too." Barlow paused, then said, "Try'n take one

of 'em alive, if you can. Mayhap he'll have some information he'd be willin' to tell us, if we asked him in jist the right way."

White Bear said, "Sounds reasonable, old chap. If we can pull it off. It might not be so easy to do."

"I know." Barlow scrabbled forward, slinking from bush to tree, trying not to present any target if the Blackfoot he had shot was still alive. The short journey seemed interminable, but he finally accomplished it. There, lying next to some blood-splattered bushes, was the warrior, a chunk of his skull missing.

Barlow sighed, partly in relief, partly in disgust, then started scanning the area again, hoping to spot either or both of the two remaining Blackfeet. He saw nothing, but moments later he heard White Bear's war cry. He smiled, figuring the Shoshoni had just removed another Blackfoot. It also worried him, though, since that severely lessened the odds of them being able to capture the fourth warrior alive.

Barlow began quietly and slowly making his way toward where he thought the Blackfoot ponies would be. He hoped he would get there before the warrior did, though he doubted it. It took him half an hour to reach the spot he thought was his target. When he got there, White Bear was sitting on a log, Buffalo lying at his feet.

"He's gone, old chap," White Bear said. "Got here just in time to see him quirtin' his bloody horse like Buffler here was ready to tear a big fat chunk of meat outta his ass. Took the rest of the bleedin' ponies with him, but never got a chance to save his mates."

"The fourth one?" Barlow asked. "There's still one unaccounted for."

"Unfortunate fellow met with an bloody fatal acci-

dent." White Bear waved a hand at his belt, in which a
fresh scalp reposed.

"Damn," Barlow snapped. "Now we gotta go find us
some more of these goddamn red devils to talk to."

"I reckon we'll do that afore long. Hell, it ain't as if
there's a shortage of those bleedin' bastards around these
here parts."

"Reckon you're right on that. But it ain't somethin' I
look forward to, hoss. These are some treacherous bastards."

"No worse than most others," White Bear said with a
grin.

"I expect you're right about that, too, hoss." Barlow
grinned. Then he said, "Let's go fill our meatbags and
git back on the trail. Mayhap we can track that bastard
and find his village."

White Bear nodded. After the battle, he could enjoy
a meal.

5

AS BARLOW RODE along that day, the fury built inside him. His irritation at not being able to capture one of the Blackfeet grew into anger, then rage. Making it all the worse was that he was becoming increasingly tired of his inability to even find Anna, let alone save her. The frustration, anger, and sense of failure ate at his innards and fed his fury.

"You have to put it out of your mind, old chap," White Bear said that night as they sat by the fire. Barlow had not said anything to him, but he knew what was wrong with his friend. "There'll be other chances to capture a bloody goddamn Blackfoot. Plenty of them. Despite their decreased numbers these days, old chap, they're still bloody bastards who live for war and the hunt. The buggers will be around in numbers we'd likely not want to see too often."

Barlow nodded. He preferred to stay silent. If he spoke, he figured that what would come out would be a torrent of curses and inanities that would accomplish nothing and probably rankle a man who had swiftly become the best friend he'd ever had.

White Bear accepted the silence but could not keep his mind from dwelling on Anna. Just before he managed to fall asleep soon afterward, he realized that what bothered Barlow was not just this morning's raid by the Blackfeet, and his and Barlow's failure at being able to capture one of them, but also the so-far fruitless three-plus-year search for his daughter. It would be enough to drive any man insane.

White Bear did not use that realization, he just kept it in mind as Barlow grew more and more morose and embittered. It helped him remain calm under his friend's increasing cantankerousness.

The Shoshoni was correct in his prediction, however, about encountering Blackfeet. Within a week, they began running into small groups of Blackfeet—usually only three or four men—out hunting or heading elsewhere to make war on some traditional enemy. The Blackfeet had no shortage of longtime enemies.

When Barlow and White Bear encountered one of these small parties, Barlow vented some of his fury, whether he and his friend initiated the attack or the Blackfeet did. But he and White Bear still made every effort to capture at least one of the enemy warriors. And when they did, Barlow became a cutthroat, viciously questioning the captured Blackfoot. He got no pleasure in these activities, but he felt them necessary and did them with detachment, as if watching someone else do it. But time after time, no matter how vicious, lengthy, or persistent his questioning of the man was, he got no helpful answers. More often than not, he ended up dispatching the warrior.

Despite his rage, Barlow was not at all comfortable with such behavior, and it began to bother him. After a few weeks of these encounters, Barlow was no closer to finding Anna. Worse, the doubts about the possibility of his never finding his daughter rose with renewed intensity and stubbornness. His rage slowly dissipated, replaced with an almost numbing despair.

Finally, Barlow called a halt for a few days. "I got to figure out jist what to do next, hoss," he explained to White Bear as they unloaded the mules.

White Bear nodded. He missed Barlow's natural cheerfulness, but he was determined to stick by his friend, even if they did pass barely a few words between them these days. He could not desert Barlow while he was in such a state, though Barlow's hopelessness was beginning to rub off on White Bear, too.

Over the next several days, Barlow began to relax minutely. Between hunting and catching up on some sleep, he slowly found some of his natural humor returning. While he was still filled with a powerful hopelessness, his spirit found a minor rebirth.

"So what do we do now, old chap?" White Bear asked nonchalantly as they lazed around their small camp one day. He hoped the question would not result in an eruption, as such questions had recently provoked.

"I ain't rightly sure, hoss," Barlow said evenly. "We cain't jist go 'round killin' every Blackfoot who cuts our trail." He paused, then added more sourly, "Well, I reckon we could, actually, but sich doin's ain't helped us none so far."

"Well, old chap," White Bear said after a considerable stretch of silence, "I'm not about to let you give up your quest just because the goin's have gotten even harder than they have been."

"You're not, eh?" Barlow knew it was a stupid thing to mutter, but he could think of nothing else to say at the moment.

"Bloody well right I'm not." White Bear paused. "I've never lost a child like this, old chap, but I can know in my heart what it would be like. And I can bloody well know that I wouldn't give up no matter how long it took to find that child of mine."

"You're a goddamn nuisance when you're right, hoss," Barlow growled. But he almost smiled. After another long pause, he added, "So, we head out again come dawn?"

White Bear nodded. "And we'll figure out what to do as we move, old chap."

"Reckon that suits this ol' chil'," Barlow agreed. He could think of nothing else to do, and he was tired of sitting. With any luck, he thought, the next Blackfoot he and White Bear captured might have the answer they sought.

They pulled out the next morning, though they were in no big hurry. For Barlow, time was still of the essence, but with no real idea of where to go, he could see no reason to press too hard. They headed northeast, ever deeper into the heart of Blackfoot country. They worked their way through the mountains, from one pass to another, through forests of pine and aspen, past ponds and across streams.

A couple of weeks later, they were following the course of the Judith River when they heard the faint sounds of a battle. Glancing at each other, they shrugged and kicked their animals into a gallop, slowing only when they knew they were getting close to the fighting. Finally, they stopped the horses and tied them to some trees. Then they moved on foot to the top of the bluff, crawling the last several yards. Buffalo lay between the two men as they peered over the edge, looking down on a small copse that backed up against the cliff a little to their left. In front of the copse, the land was mostly open, except for some boulders and an occasional tree, though the forest extended toward the northwest, with one small break from the copse. It was only the copse that appeared to be keeping the small group there from being overrun by the Blackfeet who were laying siege to it.

"Flatheads," White Bear said.

"And there's a Black Robe with them," Barlow added, pointing to a crouching figure clad in the black robe of a Jesuit missionary.

"Bloody busybody," White Bear snapped. Then he grinned a little. "Could be the reason the Blackfoot are half froze to raise hair down there."

"Hell, the Blackfeet're always half froze to raise hair on anybody who comes along, hoss. And the Flatheads've been their enemy long's anyone knows."

"I know, old chap." He ran a hand across his hair. "Well, I reckon we ought to help those bleedin' Flatheads before the Blackfeet put 'em all under."

"Reckon that won't put me out none." Barlow cocked his old Henry rifle and aimed at a Blackfoot who was hiding from the Flatheads behind a rock. A moment later, the warrior was dead, and Barlow was reloading. The Blackfeet seemed a little confused, unsure of where this attack had come from.

"You gonna take part in these doins, hoss?" Barlow questioned as he took aim again.

"Figured I'd wait till you were finished, old chap," White Bear said dryly.

"You jist cain't hit anything at this distance with them damn arrows of yours is what the problem is, hoss," Barlow said, knowing it was not the truth. He fired again, and another Blackfoot collapsed.

The remaining Blackfeet looked around in consternation.

"Time to raise hair, old chap," White Bear said quietly as he stood. He had a handful of arrows, plus one already nocked. In the time it took to blink a couple of times, he had fired all seven arrows. He hit five Blackfeet, killing two.

"Not bad, hoss," Barlow commented. He fired one more time, but missed, as the Blackfeet began shifting positions, frantically seeking where the new fire of arrows and bullets had come from. All the movement left poor targets.

"You're losin' your touch, old chap," White Bear said distractedly. The thrill of battle was beginning to sweep over him. It always did at times like this. It seemed he could do little about it but acknowledge it and let it overtake him until the battle was over.

By now, Barlow was familiar with the look White Bear now wore. And he knew what it meant. "You're aimin' to head down there, aren't you, hoss?" he questioned, though he already knew the answer.

White Bear nodded. He turned and began to hurry down the hill toward his pony. Barlow and Buffalo were close behind him. They left the pack animals there and rode swiftly off to the west, having automatically noticed that this would be the easiest way down from the bluff. It would also allow them to come up on the Blackfeet from behind.

Barlow paid no mind to Buffalo. He figured the dog would, as usual, catch up quickly once they reached the battlefield. So it was with great surprise that Barlow spotted the Newfoundland charging across the prairie from the side when he reached the site of the fight. With a quick glance, he thought he spotted a thread of a trail down the cliff that the dog must have used. He smiled at the animal's sense and courage.

But now the battle was at hand and needed his attention.

White Bear, still out in front a little, had counted coup on two Blackfeet already, touching them with his bow to show his bravery before turning and sending them to meet their maker with two swiftly fired, deadly arrows.

Barlow fired his rifle, but the lead ball did little more than kick splinters out of a boulder. He cursed and shoved the rifle away in the loop on his saddle and pulled the Colt Paterson he had taken to wearing since it had proved so effective the year before. He fired the five-shot weapon slowly, picking out his targets with care. The gun was too light to be effective at any distance.

Between the gun's lightness and him being on horseback, his firing had little effect. He hit two Blackfeet, but neither was seriously wounded. One, in fact, whirled toward him, his face angry and annoyed. The warrior snarled at him and sent two arrows flying at Barlow in the span of a heartbeat.

Barlow wasn't sure how the arrows managed to miss him, since he had had no time to react, but they did. Barlow charged toward the warrior and flung himself off the saddle into the Indian's waiting arms. They fell, Barlow atop the Blackfoot, whose back slammed against a boulder before they hit the ground. The blow on the rock combined with Barlow's weight on his chest and stomach left the warrior gasping for breath. Barlow took advantage of this and smashed the back of his elbow against the Indian's face, breaking his nose and possibly a cheekbone.

Before the Blackfoot could regain any semblance of reason and defend himself, Barlow grabbed a handy stone and pounded him to death. Barlow rose and ran a hand through his long tangle of hair.

Across the way, a Blackfoot had jumped on the back of White Bear's pony and was about to slice his throat when Buffalo raced over and leaped, knocking both warriors to the ground. The dog latched onto the Blackfoot's arm and jerked his head back and forth, tugging the Indian along the ground.

White Bear took advantage of the Newfoundland's help and quickly brained the Blackfoot with his war club, then swiftly peeled the Blackfoot's scalp free. He, too, then rose and scanned the battlefield.

The Blackfeet were fleeing. Nearly all of the dead and wounded warriors had been picked up and were being taken off. Only the ones who Barlow and White Bear had just killed were left where they lay.

The white man and the Shoshoni stayed where they were for a bit, tensely watching as the Blackfeet rode off. Until the Blackfeet were out of sight, the two were not sure that another attack would not be mounted.

Finally, though, there was relative silence. Barlow sighed in relief, and then began the laborious process of reloading the Colt Paterson. He wondered if he should keep the weapon handy. While it gave him five shots instead of two, its accuracy and stopping power were considerably less than that of the big, powerful .54-caliber muzzleloading pistols he had always carried before. He decided that decision could wait for another time.

He shoved the reloaded pistol away and headed toward his mule. The beast, the third in a line of animals named Beelzebub, was placidly cropping grass a few yards away. Barlow checked the mule over and was relieved to discover that it had not been touched by bullet or arrow. He gathered up the reins and knelt. A moment later Buffalo 2 bounded up, his curly tail waving furiously. Barlow roughly petted the dog, glad he had turned out so well.

Barlow rose and pulled himself into the saddle. While he had been petting the dog, White Bear had walked up on his pony. The light of battle still shone a little in his eyes, but it was beginning to fade.

"Well, what say we go meet those poor pilgrims hidin' in the trees, hoss?" Barlow said.

White Bear nodded. "Be interesting to hear what their bleedin' tale is, old chap."

With a glance back at the way the Blackfeet had gone, the two men turned their animals toward the stand of trees that backed up against the cliff. They had no idea of what to expect, other than there was a missionary among several Flatheads.

As they clomped toward the copse, people began filtering out of it, walking a little toward them. They stopped. Barlow and White Bear stopped, too, glanced at each other, then shrugged and pressed on. They stopped again when they were just a few feet in front of the forlorn group that had come out of the trees. The white man and the Shoshoni dismounted.

6

"I AM FATHER Sylvestre Lambert," the Black Robe said. He was a tall, reedy, determined-looking man with a firm handshake and a sanctimonious look about him.

"Will Barlow." He shook the priest's hand. "My friend there is White Bear, a Shoshoni."

White Bear and Lambert shook hands, too, the Jesuit looking rather surprised. "You are a long way from 'ome, monsieur," he said, his accent not too noticeable.

"Some, old chap," White Bear agreed. "But you're even farther from home."

"You speak ze Anglais good, *mon frere*."

White Bear nodded. He decided he did not like the priest. The Frenchman was pompous, arrogant, and, of course, overly pious. All of it went against White Bear's grain. "Better than you, old chap." There was a little bite to his words.

"Who're these others?" Barlow interjected, seeing the obstinance sparkling in White Bear's eyes. He wanted to head off a feud between the two men before it got started.

"Ah, *oui* Zese are Flat'eads."

"I know that, hoss," Barlow said, still trying to keep from letting Lambert's natural arrogance get to him. "What're their names?"

"Ah, but of course, zeir names. Ze older warrior, 'e is Black Buffalo. Zee younger one is Bull 'Eart. Black Buffalo's daughters, Little Star Woman, Raven Moon, and Far Thunder. Little Star Woman's 'usband, Painted Elk, was killed by ze Blackfeet. Zey also killed Black Buffalo's son, Gray Smoke, as well as ze 'usbands of Dancing Calf and Sky Seeker. Ze mesdames, Raising ze Lodge and Slow Sun are ze wives of Black Buffalo." His face reflected his revulsion of that notion. "Ze little ones," he added, pointing from one child to the next, "are Blue Beads, Yellow Leaf, and Lame Wing."

Barlow and White Bear nodded at each of the named people. Black Buffalo was past middle age but still held himself tall and proud, though his face was now etched with grief. Bull Heart was young, barely fourteen, but there was no doubt he was a warrior.

However, Barlow and White Bear spent most of the next few minutes gazing at Raven Moon and Far Thunder. The two were young, but not very young. Barlow wondered why neither was married. Both were short, a bit on the stocky side, but had pretty faces. They had good figures, all in all. Raven Moon's face was a little more round than Far Thunder's. The latter was a bit taller and thinner than the former. As was customary with Indian women, the two did not look at the newcomers directly, but Barlow was certain the women were appraising him and White Bear as much as they were the two women.

"How'd you come to be here?" Barlow asked.

"Well, we were visiting one of ze friendlier Blackfoot bands . . ."

"Friendlier Blackfoot bands?" Barlow interjected. "Ain't no sich goddamn thing, hoss."

"Mais oui!" Lambert began, "Zere is . . ."

"We best be on the move, old fellows," White Bear interrupted. "We can chat about this later, if you're of a mind to."

Barlow glanced at his friend and then nodded. "White Bear's right. It's gittin' a bit late, but there's still enough daylight left to make a few miles. That is, unless you folks have a powerful hankerin' to stay here and see if those damned Blackfeet decide to come back."

"Mais non!" Lambert said loudly.

"Didn't think so. I think there's a place about five miles on to the south. Think you all can make it?" Barlow looked from one person to the next. They looked worn, but not bad, and each was mounted, including the children.

"Oui!" Lambert said firmly.

Barlow looked at Black Buffalo. "You got a tongue, hoss?" he asked, both in words and with signs.

"Yep," Black Buffalo replied. "I talk. Speak damn good English, too." He tried to grin, but his still-fresh grief would not really allow it.

"Then why're you lettin' ol' Black Robe over there do all your talkin' for you?"

"Because ze Flat'eads, zey look to me as . . ."

Barlow glared at the priest. "Did I ask you anything, hoss?"

"Well, no, but . . ."

"What my mate there is tryin' to tell you, old chap," White Bear tossed in, "is to shut your yammerin' gob."

"Well?" Barlow said, looking at Black Buffalo.

The warrior shrugged. "Sometimes it easier to let him yap on." Again he tried to grin but could not quite manage it. The grief of his losses was still too fresh.

Barlow nodded, understanding. "Let's move out," he ordered.

They headed off deeper into the trees at the base of the cliff and soon entered a small rocky gorge that eventually brought them around the tall rock formation and onto a meadow. They kept moving south, not dawdling but also not using undue haste. Just under two hours later, Barlow brought them to a stop in the bend of a narrow but fast-rushing river. A grassy sward about ten yards deep ran from the river to the edge of the trees. There would be plenty of wood and water, and they would not have to worry about attack on three sides because of the river's oxbow. Across the river was a craggy peak that was too jagged and precipitous for an enemy to maneuver.

Black Buffalo, Bull Heart, and Lambert sat on a couple of large rocks while the women, and even the children to some extent, began setting up the camp. Annoyed more at the priest than the grieving Flathead warrior was, Barlow and White Bear began unloading their supplies and tending to the animals. Buffalo romped around, swimming in the river and generally enjoying himself.

"I better go see about makin' meat, old chap," White Bear said to Barlow as they worked. "We got no fresh meat, and it sure as hell doesn't look like these Flatheads have any, either."

Barlow nodded. He knew it would be more comfortable with the Flatheads if he were the one to stay here. They would, he figured, be uneasy around a hardened Shoshoni warrior. Plus there was always the fact that White Bear would hunt with a bow, thus saving Barlow's powder and ball for when it was really needed. In addition to being noiseless, it would also not alert any Blackfeet who might be lurking about.

White Bear pulled himself onto his pony and checked his quiver. He had made sure he recovered all his arrows—except the two that had snapped when they had hit rocks, of course—before joining Barlow after the battle. They were too precious and hard to make to be left behind if there was any chance of recovering them.

"Watch your hair, hoss," Barlow warned. He was a little uneasy. White Bear was a superb warrior, but when it came to a run-in with Blackfeet, that might not be enough.

White Bear grinned. "Just keep the preacher man occupied so he doesn't go sermonizing them two young women too much and turn them against havin' a lusty roll in the robes."

"Got plans, do you, hoss?" Barlow countered with a wide grin.

"Damn right. Don't you?"

"Damn right I do! That Raven Moon is as fine a woman as I've any seed," he said, staking his claim.

White Bear didn't mind. He thought Far Thunder was just as prime, though he could have—would have—easily switched allegiance. Either woman would be a catch. "Ta-ta," he said, before swinging the pony around and riding into the thick pines.

When White Bear returned less than an hour later, the camp, such as it was, was set up. Lambert had a tent, but the Flatheads had forgone their lodges. It was hot and muggy and clear, giving no reason to make the effort to erect lodges. Two fires were going, and coffee was hot. Little Star Woman and Raising the Lodge were making some kind of doughy biscuits or crackers, which did not look at all appealing to anyone.

White Bear's arrival with two deer carcasses across the pack mule was greeted enthusiastically. The Shoshoni dumped the two dead deer on the ground and then rode over to take care of his pony and the pack mule. The Flathead women hurried over and swiftly, efficiently began skinning, gutting, and butchering the deer. Soon, some meat was roasting over the fire. Other hunks were in a big iron pot, with herbs and roots the women had with them, simmering into a savory stew.

By the time White Bear was finished tending to the animals, the roasted meat was ready, and everyone sat to eat, the men at one fire, the women and children at the other. Lambert seemed a little put out.

"Somethin' eatin' at you, hoss?" Barlow asked him.

"I am used to being served, monsieur," Lambert said with a dose of indignity. "It is part of zeir training to serve ze Lord."

"Like hell," Barlow snorted. "It's more to feed your damn vanity than to serve the Lord, hoss. If you're incapable of feedin' yourself, you'll go hungry, but this ol' chil' ain't about to listen to your pompous buffler shit. Now, quit your yappin' and fill your meatbag."

Lambert looked as if he had been slapped.

It did not faze Barlow. At least not until Lambert stared for a good while longer than he should have. "What'n hell's got your nuts in a knot now, hoss?" he asked in irritation. Barlow had been looking forward to a quiet, pleasant meal. That hope was quickly fleeing.

"We did not say grace," Lambert hissed.

"Mighty observant of you, hoss," Barlow said evenly, as he calmly went on gnawing on a piece of deer meat. "But ain't no one here gonna stop you from doin' so, if you're of a mind to."

"I may be able to overlook your affronts to me, monsieur, but ze Lord will not be so kind."

"I'll worry about that when Judgment Day comes, hoss," Barlow said, letting a little of his annoyance show. "Till then, I suggest you mind your words around me."

Lambert huffed and puffed, but didn't really say anything. He finally clasped his hands together and, along with Black Buffalo and Bull Heart, began saying grace.

When they were done, Barlow asked in surprise, "You speak Latin, Black Buffler?"

Before the Flathead could answer, Lambert once again interposed himself. " 'E is very intelligent for a *sauvage*. 'E speaks Anglais, Francais, Latin, and several tongues of other *sauvages*."

"I reckon ol' Black Buffler there is more intelligent than you are, hoss," Barlow snapped. "At least he's got more goddamn manners than you. Ain't anyone ever told you it ain't polite to go puttin' words in other folks' mouths? Goddamn, you are an annoyin' critter."

"I've never been so insulted," Lambert said indignantly.

"Then it's goddamn time you was. It ain't bad enough you're fillin' these folks' heads with your gibberish, you cain't even let that ol' hoss answer a simple goddamn question." He tossed Buffalo 2 a piece of meat. The dog snatched it out of the air and gulped it down without really bothering to chew it.

"Gibberish?" Lambert snapped, almost apoplectic. "I and my brethren are bringing ze light to zese pagans. We are saving zeir souls!" The fire of the Crusaders flared in his dark eyes. "Without us, zey would be forever confined to ze flames of hell! Zey would suffer eternal damnation for zeir heathen, unenlightened ways."

"What you and your kind are doin', old chap," White Bear said harshly, "is settin' these people on the way to bleedin' extermination."

If Barlow wasn't so angry, he would have laughed at the expression that had popped unbidden onto Lambert's face. The priest was livid, choleric. So much so that he could hardly speak.

Lambert sputtered for some moments at the effrontery before he was able to form words. "I am bringing zese people ze word of God, ze only way to lead zem out of ze darkness and into God's embrace, where zey may live in light and warmth for all eternity."

White Bear could not bear to listen to such things without comment. He had a white-boy's education and had been raised for some years by an English family in Missouri, but he was still a Shoshoni, and was both proud of that and fully believed in his People's ways. Still, the education and life in the white community had supplied him with the tools to battle such foolishness, as he saw it.

"What you're bringing to these people, ye bloody papist, is the seeds of their destruction," he snapped. "You'd have them bow to a God who has far more vengeance in his heart than love of His children. A God . . ."

Barlow had to get away from the fire before he burst into laughter. White Bear had never before given any indication that he was so highly anti-Christian, or at least anti-Catholic, so Barlow figured the Shoshoni was playing the devil's advocate more because he could not stomach the overly sanctimonious Lambert than because of any real bias.

Barlow wandered to the other fire and sat between two of the children—Blue Beads, a girl of about seven, and Lame Wing, a boy of about five. "Is the meat good?" he asked in English.

The girl's mother, Little Star Woman, translated quietly.

Both children nodded enthusiastically, though their eyes remained wide in wonder at the big, broad-shouldered man. They had, of course, seen white men before, but there was something strangely powerful about Will Barlow that had them in awe.

Barlow smiled at them, though it was a little painful because it brought fresh memories of Anna to his mind. The other child—a girl of four summers or so sitting across the fire—reminded him very much of Anna. To cover his sudden discomfort, he said to Little Star Woman, "I'm sorry to hear of your loss. I hope Painted Elk died bravely."

Grief surged into Little Star Woman's eyes, but she nodded. "He die protecting us from Blackfoot. Killed three before he die."

"Were you able to bury him proper?"

Little Star Woman nodded again.

"Good." He paused. "And you others who suffered losses? Were you able to send your kin off to the after-life properly?"

There were several nods of affirmation.

Barlow wasn't sure what else to say. He wanted to find out what the marital status was of Raven Moon and Far Thunder, especially the former. But he didn't know how to broach the subject under the circumstances. He was distracted a moment later when the boy, Lame Wing, stood and moved in front of him, bravely staring him right in the eyes. Barlow did what he could to keep a straight face.

"I'm not afraid of you," the boy said in Flathead, with his mother translating.

"That's very brave of you, hoss," Barlow replied, lips itching to smile. "But you got no call to be afraid of me."

"You're not like the Black Robe."

Irritation flashed across Barlow's face, but he shoved it away. "That's a fact, boy," he said, finally grinning a little.

"I don't like him," Lame Wing said seriously.

Barlow laughed when he got the translation. "He don't shine with this ol' hoss neither, boy," he agreed.

"I like you. You're funny."

"Well, thankee, boy. I like you, too. You're a brave young feller, and I bet you'll do well in protectin' your ma."

The boy nodded gravely when he heard it in his own language, then plunked himself down again next to Barlow and grabbed a small pice of meat. Ten minutes later, he was asleep, his head on the outside of Barlow's big left thigh.

7

"I FIGURE TO stay here another day, mayhap two," Barlow said to White Bear as they spread out their sleeping robes that night.

"There a reason for that, old chap?" White Bear asked. Not that he cared all that much one way or the other.

"I'm hopin' these folks might be able to offer some helpful information about Anna. If what that damned priest said about them having visited some 'friendly' Blackfeet, mayhap they picked up somethin' we can use. Or at least mayhap point us in the right direction."

White Bear nodded, then grinned into the night. He had been a little disappointed when Barlow had not been able to learn anything about Raven Moon and Far Thunder. But if they stayed here another day or two, there would be time to learn about them and possibly entice them into the robes for some entertainment.

"That's if it don't put you out none." Barlow figured White Bear would not mind, even if for no other reason than to try his luck with one of the young women.

"It doesn't." White Bear smiled into the night again

as he stretched out atop his buffalo sleeping robe, staring at the canopy of stars and listening to the rush of the river.

"This complacency don't have anythin' to do with them two females over there, does it?" He chuckled as he lay down.

"Of course it does, old chap," White Bear said with a laugh. "I need to put old Nebuchadnezzar out to grass, old chum. And damn soon."

"What the hell does that mean?" Barlow asked with a chuckle.

"It means, mate, that I have one hell of a need to engage in sexual intercourse."

Barlow burst into laughter. "This ol' hoss could be usin' a dose of the same medicine, boy. Sure as hell." It took him a while to fall asleep. The hope that Raven Moon—or even Far Thunder—would show up and join him was strong. He wondered if White Bear was having the same thoughts. But it never happened, and eventually sleep overtook him.

When Barlow awoke, the area was covered in mist rising thickly from the river, weaving through the trees. He rose and stood there a moment, breathing deeply of the fresh, moist air. He could see little, and it was almost impossible to tell that dawn was on them. A short distance away, he could see a dim amber glow, and knew it was one of the fires. He headed toward the glimmer, stumbling once or twice on loose stones. At the fire, he knelt and began stoking it, nursing it into flames.

He jerked in surprise and reached for his knife, at the touch of a hand on his shoulder. He blew out a breath and relaxed when he realized it was Raven Moon. He smiled and was heartened when it was returned.

"I do that," she said quietly.

"You sure? I can handle this."

"I sure," Raven Moon said firmly.

Barlow nodded and rose. He started to turn away but then decided he needed to strike up a conversation with her. "Your husband's not along on this journey?" he asked.

Raven Moon shook her head as she knelt and worked on the fire. "He die. Three winters ago."

"I'm sorry to hear that," Barlow lied. Not that he was unsympathetic, but knowing she had been a widow for a fair amount of time was encouraging.

Raven Moon shrugged. "It long time ago."

"Why ain't you married again?" Barlow asked, surprised. "A fine lookin' woman like you should have heaps of men courtin' her all the time."

"Many have," she said with another shrug. She glanced up at him and smiled. "Not find any I . . . like."

"You got anything against a wild and woolly white-eyes courtin' you?"

"No," Raven Moon said resolutely, looking up at him, even briefly staring into his eyes.

"That shines with this ol' chil'," Barlow allowed. "How about your sister, Far Thunder? She got a husband back in the village or somethin'?"

"No. He die, too. Same time." She suddenly looked angry, but Barlow didn't notice.

"Would she be interested in the attentions of . . ."

He was startled into silence when Raven Moon rose and shoved past him. "I busy," she said.

"Hey, now, wait a damn minute here," Barlow said, grabbing her arm and holding her lightly. He realized what the problem was. "I ain't interested in your sister. I was jist gonna ask if you think she'd mind the attentions of a certain Shoshoni."

Raven Moon stared up at his face, as if searching for

an answer. Apparently she found it, and she smiled. "I think she like."

"Good," Barlow said, grinning hugely.

"Yes, good." Raven Moon grinned and went back to working on the fire.

Barlow strolled off, heading toward the river. In just a few minutes the sun had risen a bit, and the fog was a little less thick. He could almost see the edge of the water—once he was right on top of it. He squatted and dipped his hands in the cold water, then splashed his face. It was an eye-opening jolt.

Behind him, the camp was waking. The children were beginning to play, making a racket, as children everywhere seemed to do. Barlow heard Father Lambert saying his morning Rosary. The women set about heating up coffee and warming stew or roasting meat. Soon the aromas of the latter drifted over Barlow, and he smiled. The mist had risen a little more, and he figured it would not last more than another hour before it was completely burned away.

Barlow rose and strolled back to the fire. Black Buffalo, Bull Heart, and White Bear were already there. He took a seat, and with a smile of thanks took the bowl of stew and cup of coffee that Raven Moon handed him.

"Well, old chap," White Bear said quietly, "looks like you've been busy impressin' that young lady."

"If you wasn't sleepin' till damn near the noon hour, you might be able to court somebody, too."

"You probably paid for her attentions with a heap of foofaraw."

Barlow laughed a little. "Like either of us has any foofaraw." When the laughter faded a moment later, he said, "I did find out that Far Thunder is a widow and likely wouldn't mind some attentions, even from the likes of some broke-down ol' Shoshoni."

White Bear's eyebrows raised. "You speakin' true, old chap?"

Barlow nodded.

"Well, that shines, it does!"

"What does, White Bear?" Lambert asked as he sat nearby, straightening out his long robes as he did.

"Somethin' you wouldn't approve of, old chap," White Bear said evenly.

Barlow hid a grin behind his tin mug of coffee. The priest and the Shoshoni had argued considerably past dark the night before about the missionary's influence— both good and bad, of course—on the Flatheads. What he didn't know was how the two men felt about each other after that. White Bear seemed to be as calm and reasonable as ever, bearing no overt ill will. He wasn't sure about Lambert, however.

"Zere is little zat you—or your friend over zere—do zat I approve of, White Bear."

"Then I bloody well reckon you don't know what we were bloomin' talkin' about then, old chap."

Lambert bit back another retort, and instead looked around angrily. "Where are those women?"

"Busy, hoss," Barlow sad dryly. "Git your own vittles."

"But they served you."

"Well, one of 'em did. I reckon it's because I treat 'em with a little respect. Somethin' mayhap you should try."

White Bear was already reaching for meat and poured himself coffee. By now, Black Buffalo had finished eating and was puffing on an old clay pipe. Bull Heart, with a teenager's appetite, was still eating. Finally, Lambert served himself, his annoyance at it evident on his florid face and by his stiff movements.

As they ate, Barlow said to White Bear, "I reckon we

ought to take us a little look-see around this mornin', hoss."

"You suspect something, old chap?"

Barlow shook his head. "Nah, not really. I jist want to make sure none of the goddamn Blackfeet're still lurkin' about. Once I know that, we can spend a bit of time here talkin' with Black Buffler's people and see if we can learn anything that might help find Anna."

"Who is zis Anna?" Lambert asked.

Barlow glared at him, then realized it was a reasonable question.

"My daughter, hoss. We're lookin' for her."

"What 'appened?"

"I'll explain later. Right now I want to git movin' and see that we'll be safe here for a day or two."

"But, Monsieur Barlow . . ."

Barlow tossed his bowl and cup down, rose, and walked away, ignoring the priest. The anger had popped up again, and he did not want to give it vent right now. The priest might be a pompous, sanctimonious man, but his questions were not unreasonable. Barlow just did not want to deal with them right now.

White Bear slid silently up as Barlow was saddling Beelzebub and began readying his pony. Within minutes, they were riding through the trees, towing two unloaded pack mules with them. Buffalo 2 loped along, weaving his own trail through the tree trunks and all, never getting more than a few yards away.

They crossed the river half a mile away and moved out around the peak across from their camp and headed northwest, up a gently sloping hillside covered with aspens, then out of the trees and onto a great, wide plain. They stopped and scanned the horizon, seeing no sign of Blackfeet anywhere. There was a fair-sized herd of mountain buffalo out there, though.

"I think I got me a hankerin' for some buffler meat, ol' hoss," Barlow said with a grin.

"My thinkin', too, old chap. It's been a bleedin' long time since we've filled ourselves on some bloomin' good hump meat."

Barlow nodded. "I reckon we out to go around them buffler for the time being and check out what's beyond that next big stand of trees yonder. I reckon if we don't seen no sign of Blackfeet then, we'll be free of them critters for at least a spell."

White Bear nodded, and they moved off.

By the time they determined that there were no Blackfeet in the vicinity and had ridden back to the valley where the buffalo awaited, it was past noon. They stopped within twenty yards of the herd and looked it over again, subconsciously picking out a prime cow. Then, grinning at each other, they kicked their mounts into a run, leaving the pack animals were they were.

Beelzebub raced ahead for all it was worth, directed by Barlow toward a fat cow. The herd suddenly realized something was wrong and bolted. Barlow moved the mule closer to the cow, knowing he didn't have long before the buffalo outran Beelzebub. They pulled up alongside at a full gallop. Barlow lowered his rifle until the muzzle was only inches from the buffalo's thick hide. He fired.

The cow tumbled on its knees and skidded along for yards before it tumbled to a halt in a bloody, dusty heap.

Barlow pulled Beelzebub to a stop a few yards away and patted the beast's sweaty neck. He rode slowly back toward the buffalo, noting that White Bear was already dismounted and was butchering the cow he had slain. Barlow was soon emulating his friend, hating the heat of the day that made this an onerous job.

They took only the tongue, hump meat, and the thick

fleece of fat from the hump. White Bear eagerly ate the raw liver of one, but Barlow had never been able to really cotton to that. He did, however, make sure Buffalo 2 had a good portion of organ meats.

White Bear rode up soon after, having retrieved the pack animals. He left one with Barlow and took the other with him. The two men packed the meat, which was wrapped in pieces of bloody hide they had sliced off, onto the pack mules and soon were riding off again, heading toward their camp. Buffalo plodded along, tongue lolling in the heat.

It was midafternoon before they rode back into the camp. Lambert was saying Mass, with Black Buffalo, Bull Heart, the women and the children all appearing to be attentive. Barlow shook his head in annoyance, then shrugged. It was not his business, and he did not think it would affect any possible carnal relationship between he and Raven Moon. She certainly hadn't indicated anything of the sort.

They unloaded the meat near the women and children's fire, then went back to tend to the animals. Once finished, both men headed for the river. While Barlow was not fond of bathing—indeed, thought it bad for the body—he figured a good dunking would not be a bad idea, considering how sweaty and covered in buffalo blood he was.

Since his clothes needed cleaning as much as he did, he headed into the river fully clothed after having dropped his weapons and belt on the shore. The cold water felt good at first but swiftly chilled him. He hurried out, White Bear's mocking laughter ringing in his ears. The afternoon's heat soon dried him, and he relaxed with a pipe and mug of coffee, sitting with his back against a rock, under the trees.

White Bear joined him not long afterward, and they

listened to Lambert's dull voice droning on with the Mass.

"I wonder if that ol' hoss ary gits tired of hearin' hisself talk," Barlow mused.

"His kind never does, old chap."

"Reckon that's a fact."

Soon enough the priest's official sermonizing for the day ended, much to Barlow and White Bear's relief. Before long, the men were all sitting around one fire, having a meal of rich buffalo meat. And when they were done and smoking their pipes, Barlow said, "Now, Black Buffler, how's about you tell us jist what you and your people're doin' out here dealin' with the goddamn Blackfeet."

8

"WE GO TO visit some Blackfeet. Friends," Black Buffalo said.

"Father Lambert said that before—that you were visiting friendly Blackfeet," Barlow interjected. "This ol' chil' ain't ever heard of sich a thing as friendly Blackfeet. Not with Americans. Not with Flatheads, not with Crows or Bannocks or Shoshonis."

"Zere is a small group zat . . ." Lambert started. He stopped when Barlow glared at him.

"There's a band of Blackfeet called the Small Robes," Black Buffalo said. "They friends with my People for many winters. Other Blackfeet don't like that they are our friends."

"I can see why," Barlow muttered. "That goes against the grain in a big way, I reckon."

Black Buffalo nodded. "The Small Robes ask us to bring Black Robes to them. They want a mission so they can learn the spirit talking of them." He sighed and puffed at his pipe a little. "I think it's bad idea," he finally continued.

"Now, Black Buffalo," Lambert chided harshly, "you know zat we wish only to bring God's light to ze Small Robes, as well as ze Flat'eads."

"Shut your gob, mate," White Bear said. "If we want any information from you, we'll let you know. Go ahead, Black Buffalo."

"The Black Robes—Pere Lambert here and Pere Renaud—came to our village not long ago to visit, and I tell them about the Small Robes' request. They said they will go if I will take them. Pere Renaud will stay with the Small Robes, while Pere Lambert will come back to our village."

"That's where this Father Renaud is now?" Barlow asked. "With the Small Robes?"

"*Non*!" Lambert snapped. " 'E is dead at ze 'ands of ze Blackfeets. Ze 'eathens, zey kill him and . . ."

"We get the idea, hoss," Barlow said. "You seem angry at that, but you don't seem to be grievin' much over the loss of your partner."

" 'E is with ze Lord, our God, now. 'Ow can I grieve for zat? It is what we look forward to, *mon fils*. And 'e was doing ze Lord's work when 'e died. No, zere is no reason for me to grieve over 'im. I envy 'im in some ways because 'e is in 'eaven. I wish I were zere with him."

"We can arrange that, old chap," White Bear muttered so quietly that only Barlow heard him.

Fighting back a smile, Barlow asked, "Don't you miss him?"

"Ah, *oui*. But to allow grief and ze sense of loss to hinder my work with ze Flat'eads or any other 'eathens would be to question God's reasoning, and I cannot do zat."

Barlow nodded. It made as much sense as anything

else Lambert ever said. "So, Black Buffalo," he asked, "what happened then?"

"We took Black Robes to see our friends. The Small Robes seemed pleased with what the priests had to say to 'em. After feastin' and celebratin' for a couple days, they ask Pere Renaud to stay and teach 'em the ways of the white-eyes' God."

"Much to this Renaud's delight, I expect," Barlow said dryly.

Black Buffalo nodded. "Wanted to start savin' souls right off. He was plannin' baptisms and Masses and all . . ."

"But somethin' stopped him?" White Bear questioned, knowing the answer even as he asked.

Black Buffalo nodded sadly, his grief returning. "The goddamn Blackfoot come. Told the Small Robes they just come to trade and to talk."

"Not too happy when they saw the Black Robes there, were they?" Barlow asked sarcastically.

"No," Black Buffalo responded flatly. "It not bad enough the Small Robes are friends of the People, and we were there. But to have us bringing Black Robes there made them paint their faces black against us. They left right away, but we knew they'd be back. Wasn't long either. They attacked hard and fast."

"That when Renaud went under?" Barlow asked.

Black Buffalo nodded. "Damn fool went out with his beads and his holy book, thinkin' his medicine could stop the damned Blackfeet." He shook his head at the folly of it all. It was then that he had decided the Black Robes' talk was not for him. The Black Robes had come with words of their all-powerful God. Their promises of a glorious world where those who believed in their God and the Christ child fell now on deaf ears, once Black Buffalo had seen how little power the Black Robes' words had. There had been no divine retribution for the slaughter of their God's appointed representative. If it had happened to his own people—which it had—Black Buffalo would have believed that that person or someone close to him had broken some taboo and turned their medicine bad. But the Black Robes had ridiculed such notions and led the Flatheads to believe that the Black Robes lived always in a state of grace and that the Flat-head people should emulate them in all ways. But that could not be true, Black Buffalo thought. Not after what he had just seen. He would allow Lambert to continue living in the village and do his proselytizing if the priest still wanted to—and if others in the village wanted it. But he would not take part, and he would spread word of the fallibility of the Black Robes.

The Flathead leader sighed. "Painted Bull, Swift Bear, Ten Crows, and Broken Hump fought bravely. So did young Bull Heart. All . . ."

"You the bravest of all, Grandfather," Bull Heart interjected quietly but forcefully.

Black Buffalo smiled sadly and nodded. "All but Bull Heart and me die. Between the people and the Small Robes, we drove the Blackfeet off. We know they be back. We know they hadn't run off. Just were regroupin'. Didn't know how long. We buried our people swiftly and made ready to leave. The damned Blackfeet wait two suns before coming back. They think they could fool us into lettin' our guard down. But we didn't. When the damned Blackfeet did return, the Small Robes fled, hoping to draw Blackfeet after them, so we could escape."

"Didn't work, though, did it, old chap?" White Bear asked softly.

Black Buffalo shook his head. "Blackfeet not all fooled. Most chased the Small Robes, but some of them come for us. They catch us soon. We hold them off, not losin' any more people, but things was lookin' mighty bad, and we weren't sure we could hold off much longer."

"That's when we come along and found you?" Barlow asked.

Black Buffalo nodded. "You and White Bear bring big medicine for us," he said firmly, casting a disparaging glance at Lambert. "Not like the Black Robes, who talk of powerful medicine, but have none."

"Why'n't you try'n stop them Blackfeet with your holy words and such, hoss?" Barlow asked Lambert, knowing the priest would have no good answer.

Lambert opened his mouth to respond, but then slapped it shut. How could he explain to such Godless barbarians? They would understand nothing of what he preached. They were incapable of it, either the red savages or the white one. He looked off into the distance, showing his disdain for Barlow and the others—and for the impudent question.

Barlow managed to keep the smile off his face. He had never liked preachers or priests, those holier-than-thou types who as often as not turned out to be as sinful as everyone else but who tried to cover over their misdeeds with scripture.

"So what now, old chap?" White Bear asked.

"We go home," Black Buffalo said.

"Gonna be a hard march, ol' hoss," Barlow said. "I reckon them damned Blackfeet're gonna come lookin' for you again, if they ain't already."

Black Buffalo nodded. "There is nothin' else to do. We must get back to the people. We'll do it however best we can." He stopped when Bull Heart leaned over and whispered urgently into his ear for a few moments. Then Black Buffalo sat, thinking, eyes closed against the bright sunlight. His pipe, which had gone out, was still clenched between his teeth, and it bobbled a little. Finally, his eyes opened and he pulled the pipe out of his mouth. He looked at his grandson and nodded, then looked back toward Barlow and White Bear.

He did not like having to do this, but it was, he had decided, the only way. "Will you two help us?" he asked gravely.

"Help you?" Barlow asked, sure he knew what Black Buffalo was asking, but wanting to be certain.

"Help us to get back to our village." Black Buffalo was ashamed at seeming so weak in front of these others. But he had the welfare of the women and children in his hands, and they had to come first.

"I don't know, Black Buffalo," Barlow said quietly. "We got plans, things to do."

"You would leave us to ze tender mercies of ze Blackfeet?" Lambert asked. He saw a ray of hope here, a way of having a much better chance of getting back to Flathead country, where they would be safe, and he could continue converting the savages in peace.

Seeing Barlow's hesitation, the priest added, "You just said so yourself zat zey will come after us again. And we are almost 'elpless. We 'ave only two warriors, and all ze women and children. Ze Blackfeet would cut us to pieces."

Barlow thought it over. He hated the priest, but he had nothing against Black Buffalo and Bull Heart. He glanced over at the knot of women and children, most of whom seemed to know what they were talking about and were watching in expectation—or fear. It was a sorry looking bunch, all in all, as far as being able to travel safely while bands of bloodthirsty Blackfeet were out after their hair.

"What do you think, old chap?" White Bear prodded him.

"I'm thinkin' of Anna," Barlow said flatly. He hated to refuse the Flatheads, but Anna was foremost in his mind.

"Maybe we can get these here chaps to help," White Bear suggested.

"You talk of this Anna before," Black Buffalo interrupted. "Are you lookin' for her?"

Barlow nodded. When he looked at White Bear, the Shoshoni chucked his chin toward the women and children. Barlow looked over his shoulder. Standing away from the group a little was Yellow Leaf, who seemed to be staring straight at him—maybe even straight through him. He fought back an involuntary shudder. Yellow Leaf was about the same age Anna would now be. A jagged pain pierced his heart. Anna was always foremost in his thoughts, but she had become something ethereal, almost having lost some reality for him. But Yellow Leaf was here, and alive, and real. He could not bring himself to leave her—or the others—to the likely clutches of the Blackfeet.

"We'll do it," Barlow said firmly.

"*Bon*!" Lambert interjected. He was almost beaming.

Black Buffalo simply nodded. He was relieved, though still bothered by the thought that he had had to ask for help. He turned and whispered to Bull Heart, who sauntered toward the women and children, trying with all his might to keep himself from bursting into a run.

The men were all silent. Barlow relit his pipe and puffed, wondering where Anna was and just when he would get her back. Despite the etherealness of his search these days, he was no less certain now than he was the day she had been taken that he would get her back safely. He comforted her in his mind, and sent the words outward and upward on the puffs of smoke from his pipe, hoping they would reach her.

Somewhat comforted by that notion, Barlow relaxed a bit, and his mind turned to the Flatheads. There would be some benefits to making this side trip to the Flathead village—there would be time to spend with Raven Moon. He wanted to find Anna more than anything, but he was a man with a normal man's needs, and they would now be met, he figured. He glanced toward the other fire and caught a glimpse of Raven Moon. Yes, he decided, this would not be unpleasant at all.

"Tell me about Anna," Black Buffalo finally said, startling Barlow out of his increasingly carnal reverie. "You say she is your daughter?"

"Yep, that's right. My daughter. She was took from me by a band of bastards known as Umpquas, way out by the big water to the west. They kilt my wife and my little boy and made off with Anna. The infernal bastard who took her lost her in a game of hand to White Bear here."

Black Buffalo's eyes widened, and he glanced from one man to the other in surprise. Barlow nodded. "I went lookin' for him to put him under and take my Anna back. But he didn't know she was took from me and weren't happy when he found out she was. But by that time he'd been tricked out of her by some devilish sons of bitches, who planned to sell her and a heap of other young'uns to the Blackfeet. Trouble was, the Blackfeet either weren't interested in dealin' or those boys jist turned Bug's Boys' hearts black against 'em somehow. The Blackfeet jist made wolf bait out of them boys and took the children. That's why we're out here—lookin' for Anna amongst the goddamn Blackfeet."

"Do you know who has her?" Black Buffalo asked.

Barlow shook his head, the sadness returning. "We been out here a long spell lookin' and lookin'. We've talked to a number of Bug's Boys and gotten nothin'."

"Talked to?" Lambert interjected. "I thought you hated ze Blackfeet and zat zey would 'ave nothing to do with you."

"They didn't exactly volunteer to parley with us, hoss," Barlow said flatly. "They needed a bit of encouragement."

"You tortured zem?" Lambert asked in horror.

"We asked 'em questions. If they were reluctant to offer any answers, we encouraged 'em is all."

"Zat is sinful, *mon fils*. And it didn't work either, did it?"

"Nope. Didn't work. But it has worked before. And it'll work again. We jist need to find the feller who knows somethin'. And sooner or later, by Christ, I am gonna find that ol' hoss."

"You compound your sinfulness, monsieur. Ze Lord will hold zese things against your account when Judgment Day arrives."

Barlow shrugged. "No matter, hoss," he said harshly. "I'm gonna hold it against Him that my Anna's been took away and spirited from one band of red devils to another. He has a heap of answerin' to do."

Lambert was aghast at the blasphemy. "Such talk," he said, trying to keep calm, "will guarantee you spend all eternity in ze fires of 'ell."

Barlow shrugged again. "After some of the doin's I been through, hoss, hell don't hold no worries for me."

Still appalled, Lambert shook his head. "Did you ever think," he finally said slowly, "zat you cannot find *votre fille* because you 'ave forsaken the Lord? 'Ave you ever thought zat perhaps she was taken from you because you 'ave neglected God and his Son, Jesus?"

"That's goddamn ridiculous, hoss," Barlow snapped, grinding his teeth. He shoved up and moved off, a concerned Buffalo 2 bouncing around him, watching his master carefully.

9

WHITE BEAR FOUND Barlow sometime later. Barlow was sitting on a log along the river about fifty yards from camp, seemingly oblivious to everything around him.

" 'Ello, old chap," White Bear said, taking a seat on a rock a few feet from Barlow, facing him at a slight angle. When he got no response, he asked, "You havin' regrets about offerin' to help these folks?"

Barlow shrugged.

"It's the right thing, old chap."

"I reckon." Barlow sighed. "You think there's anything to what that damned priest said, White Bear?" he suddenly asked.

"What's that, old chap? That Anna's capture and such is somehow your fault because you don't believe in God the way that bloody damn fool does?"

Barlow nodded.

"That's a pack of codswallop, mate. If that's true, how do you explain that other bleedin' priest gettin' rubbed out by the Blackfeet the other day? Besides, I expect you've said more'n your share of prayers since you started lookin' for Anna. Maybe not the way old bleedin' Lambert thinks is proper. But it don't matter what that bugger thinks. He ain't no more the Great Spirit's messenger here than I am, old chap."

"You think?"

White Bear nodded. Having been raised in both his native religion and that of the white man, he considered his own religion superior. He was particularly anti-Catholic, seeing how his white home had been Anglican. That was exacerbated by Lambert's overly sanctimonious attitude.

"I hope you're right, hoss," Barlow said flatly.

"I am," White Bear replied with confidence. "Now, let's get back over by the fire there. I think old Black Buffalo has somethin' up his sleeve."

"About what?" Barlow asked, surprised.

"About Anna, I think. Now that he knows of your quest, maybe he's thought of somethin' that'll help. Maybe he heard somethin' from those bloody Small Robes."

"That'd be nice for a change," Barlow admitted. He rose. "Well, let's go, hoss, and see what he's got to say."

Black Buffalo, Bull Heart, and Lambert were still sitting around their fire, but now the women were hovering around, serving bowls of food and coffee. Barlow and White Bear took their places and gratefully accepted the food and drink. Barlow was well aware of the warm look Raven Moon beamed at him as she served him. He returned it with a look of heat in his eyes.

As they ate, Barlow said, "So, Black Buffalo, White Bear tells me you can maybe help me find Anna."

"Maybe can," Black Buffalo said solemnly. He set his bowl down. "I'll go find the Small Robes and see if they can help. Maybe they know something. Maybe they hear something. Most Blackfeet hate the Small Robes, but sometimes they peaceful, trade, and talk. Maybe they know of something from the other Blackfeet."

Barlow's eyes burned with interest and hope. "You'd do that?" he asked, almost afraid as if this was a dream.

Black Buffalo nodded. "You save my people. You agree to help us back to the village. Now I help you, if I can."

"I'd be mighty obliged, Black Buffalo," Barlow said earnestly.

"One condition," the Flathead said. "You and White Bear watch over my people while I'm gone."

Barlow agreed readily. Since he and the Shoshoni were to help the Flatheads get back to their country, they would not be going anywhere else for a while anyway. "When'll you leave, hoss?" he asked.

"First light."

Barlow nodded. "Reckon me and you ought to be doin' a bit more huntin' today, White Bear," he said.

"I'm coopered, old chap. Why . . ."

"You're what?" Barlow and Lambert asked at the same time.

"Worn out, mates. Reckon them wounds of mine ain't as healed up as I might've been thinkin'. Why don't you take the boy with you, old chap?" White Bear said, pointing to Bull Heart.

Barlow looked at the youth. "You want to go make meat with me, boy?" he asked, not at all unkindly.

Bull Heart nodded enthusiastically. He was fascinated by the white man, though he wasn't sure why. He'd seen white men before, but never one quite like Will Barlow. He would like to talk with him some. This seemed like a perfect opportunity.

"All right, boy, go on and git your pony. I'll be along directly." He looked at the Flathead leader. "That's all right with you, ain't it, Black Buffalo?" he asked.

The Flathead nodded.

"We'll be back in a spell," Barlow said, rising. He strode off, heading for Beelzebub. He saddled the mule swiftly and soon was riding out of the camp. Bull Heart rode proudly alongside him, his bow unstrung now and resting in a sheath attached to his quiver, which was full of arrows. Each man held the rope to a pack mule. Buffalo went along, too, keeping his own pace and making his own trail as he saw fit.

They returned to the camp more than two hours later. Loaded on the mules were two partially butchered elk carcasses. Each elk had been brought down by a single perfectly placed arrow fired by Bull Heart. Barlow was impressed with the young man's skill. The two of them had done the butchering, chatting quietly about nothing in particular as they worked.

Bull Heart decided that one reason he liked the former mountain man was his generally easygoing nature. But even more than that was the fact that he was not fond of Father Sylvestre Lambert. Bull Heart had decided even before Father Renaud's death at the hands of the Blackfeet that Lambert was not quite the man he claimed to be. He had noticed that Lambert did not really seem to have the courage of his convictions. Whereas Renaud had believed enough in his faith that he thought it would keep him safe from the Blackfeet, Lambert had never shown similar inclinations.

The fresh meat was well received in the camp, and Black Buffalo praised Bull Heart for his abilities once Barlow had related how the young man had been responsible. Before long, everyone was eating fresh roasted elk and downing hot coffee.

The men talked until dark, trying hard to keep their conversation from veering into areas that would spark arguments. They succeeded fairly well, with a debate breaking out only a few times.

Finally, Barlow rose. "It's robe time for this chil'," he announced. He turned and headed for his sleeping robes. White Bear was only moments behind him. They spread their robes out quietly, said good-night, and stretched out.

Barlow kept his eyes open for a while. He was hoping that Raven Moon would show up. She had been warm and friendly all day, and he had thought she would be there. But he waited and waited. Finally he closed his eyes and tried to sleep. Maybe tomorrow night, he thought. Or maybe she wasn't interested. But he could not accept that. And after a while of getting nowhere near sleep, he rose and padded off into the darkness, walking rather silently for such a big, bulky man.

So quietly did he move that Raven Moon, who was waiting behind some brush, didn't hear him until he almost stepped on her hand. He stopped at her startled squeak. "Raven Moon?" he whispered.

"Yes," she responded in kind.

Barlow knelt and reached out for the woman. She came willingly into his arms. "What're you doing out here like this?"

"I wait for right time to come to you," she said simply.

"Well, gal, I been waitin' fer quite a spell for you to come to me. I about give up on that when I decided I had to come find you if I could."

"You find me." Raven Moon giggled a little.

"Reckon I did at that." He rose, tugging her gently up with him. "Are you ready?" he asked, his voice thick with desire.

"Yes," she breathed. Her dark eyes gleamed in the moonlight.

They strolled into the trees, Barlow unerringly leading her to his sleeping robes. He gathered up the otter-fur bedding and carried it off another ten or fifteen feet, so he and Raven Moon would not be too close to White Bear. He spread the soft, plush robe down and turned toward the Flathead woman.

She waited rather demurely. She seemed shy without being coy. In the moonlight, lust burned in her eyes, but she still carried an air of reserve about her. Barlow wondered if perhaps her religious indoctrination by Father Lambert had somehow undermined her sexuality.

Raven Moon smiled, and Barlow reached out and pulled her to him, kissing her hard. She returned it with equal fervor, and Barlow's doubts about her lustiness began to dissipate. With Raven Moon's willing help, Barlow peeled off her dress and then shucked his own clothes. Naked, they stretched out on the plush fur. Barlow began running one hand over Raven Moon's body, delighting in the smoothness of her skin and the murmurs of pleasure his ministrations elicited from her.

He swung a leg over her and rose until he was straddling Raven Moon and brought his other hand into action, stroking her lightly from her forehead to her upper thighs. She smiled almost dreamily, and her hair spread out on the sleeping robe in a tangled dark mass that was virtually invisible in the darkness. It could be seen only where the moonlight glinted off its ebony.

As Barlow reacted to Raven Moon's increasingly squirming body, he took the time to gently knead her breasts and tweak her nipples, pulling them lightly into sharp little points that seemed to beckon for even more attention.

Barlow was pleased to oblige and soon replaced his hands on her breasts with his lips, tongue and mouth, teasing her succulent flesh and her sensitive nipples. She murmured more steadily as heat spread through her, and her body began to writhe more insistently.

Her hands went up and locked around the back of Barlow's neck, and she held his mouth in place on one of her breasts as her buttocks wriggled more and more. She finally let his head go, and he looked up and grinned at her. Soon he was marking a trail between her breasts with small nibbling kisses. He pushed himself backward a little, continuing his path of light kisses down to her navel and further. Gently shoving her legs open with his knees, he lifted her buttocks up so that her womanhood was fully accessible to his face. And he made good use of his tongue and lips.

Within moments, Raven Moon reached her peak, gasping loudly as pleasure rolled over her. Waves of ecstasy ebbed then rose again as Barlow continued delighting her woman's flesh and the secret pleasure button hidden within the velvet folds. Again and again, pleasure came and faded, like the tides. With each peak came a panting rush of air and a muttered expression in Flathead.

Finally, Barlow gave Raven Moon a break, setting her buttocks down and then moving his body up over hers, until he could kiss her hard and deep. Though somewhat out of breath from the bliss Barlow had just given her, Raven Moon responded enthusiastically, wrapping her forearms around his neck so she could keep him where she wanted him for a while. Which she did, with great joy.

Raven Moon finally had to release him, though, and he moved backward a little, resting on his shins between her legs. "You ready?" he asked, smiling broadly.

"Much ready. Lots ready," Raven Moon agreed.

As Barlow learned forward onto his hands again, Raven Moon grasped his manroot and guided him into her. He slid easily into her, aided by her ecstasy-induced wetness. He paused there, buried to the hilt in her, letting the warm sensations wash through his entire body.

Finally he began to move. Balancing on knees and hands, he drove easily in and out of her at a slow, steady pace. She soon matched his tempo, her hips rising and falling in perfect cadence.

Soon, however, Raven Moon again began a short climb toward another climax, and that threw off her rhythm. Not that it mattered to either of them at that point. Raven Moon was suddenly bouncing wildly on the sleeping robe, her breathing ragged, coming in spurts. Her nostrils flared and almost pulsated as a new pinnacle shook her from head to foot.

Barlow had to stop moving for some moments to let Raven Moon come down from the peak on which she had just crested. But within seconds, he was sliding in and out of her again, and Raven Moon almost instantly started matching his pace. Their concerted movements soon had both of them gliding up the short hill toward climax, and it happened to each within moments of each other, a powerful, body-and-soul-shaking explosion that began at their conjoined groins and sparked outward until it overtook every muscle and tendon.

Barlow had trouble breathing and was gulping air like a fish flopping on a riverbank. He pulled himself free and squatted back on his heels, blowing like a bull about to charge. His great chest heaved and his mouth was dry.

Raven Moon looked up at him, a little concerned, but she was having enough trouble with her own lack of oxygen to be too worried. She was relieved, however, when he at last stretched out beside her and took her in his arms. He appeared to her to have caught up on his breathing and was becoming quite relaxed.

"Damn, woman," Barlow said, still behind on his breathing.

"You damn good, too," Raven Moon said with a smile.

Barlow nodded into the darkness. He was asleep seconds later, content in having Raven Moon wrapped around his bulk.

He was even happier when he awoke shortly before dawn with Raven Moon still cuddled in his embrace. She awoke moments after he did, and smiled at him. "You ready for another?" he asked.

Raven Moon nodded, grinning wildly. "Much ready."

Barlow lay on his back and pulled the woman atop of him. She was a wisp compared with his great size. But she was fierce enough as she playfully attacked him. And she held her own as their bodies tangled and writhed and sweated and finally exploded in a climax that left them each gasping for air once again.

Barlow dozed off soon after, unaware of a well-satisfied, quite happy Raven Moon leaving to tend to her duties.

10

FATHER LAMBERT WAS livid when he finally arrived and took his place by the fire that morning. He glared at Barlow, and when Raven Moon came around to serve food and coffee, he glowered at her, too. Barlow didn't mind Lambert's scrutiny all that much, but he was not about to let Raven Moon undergo the priest's withering, silent condemnation.

"Somethin' stuck in your craw, hoss?" Barlow asked evenly. "You look like you jist swallered a porkypine."

It was several moments before Lambert could speak, and when he finally did, the words were clipped with anger and revulsion. "It is not bad enough, monsieur, zat you will be consigned to ze fires of 'ell for all eternity for your adulterous ways. But to sully zis fine young woman, mon dieu, zat is unthinkable." He was positively choleric.

"Well, now, I reckon you might see it that way, hoss," Barlow said in a tone intended to irritate the priest. "But me'n Raven Moon here don't. And we'd be obliged if you was to keep your thoughts on the matter to yourself."

"I cannot do zat, monsieur. *Mais non*! It is ze devil's 'and at work 'ere, and I must make you see zat. You must stop zis sinful behavior and repent. You must atone, too, for leading zis unsaved young woman down ze path of depravity."

"Well, hoss, you can pray for us all you're of a mind to, if you think that'll help. But you jist stay away from Raven Moon and me." Barlow looked at Raven Moon and jerked his head slightly toward the other fire.

The woman smiled at him, nodded, and left, heading for where the children and most of the other women were.

Barlow stood. "Jist remember what I said, hoss," he growled. He thumped off, anger building in him.

White Bear had watched the exchange with a combination of humor and irritation. He thought the exchange funny, but the fact that Barlow had had carnal knowledge of Raven Moon only a few yards away while he had been alone was highly aggravating. He glanced at Far Thunder and thought she flashed him a small but inviting smile. He decided he would have to see if his thought was right. And soon.

Barlow decided to check the mules as a way of letting his anger dissipate. All the animals seemed in fine condition—their shoes were in good shape and their backs unblemished by the packs and pack saddles. He untied the mules and moved them a few feet away, allowing them better grazing. By then, Barlow's anger had faded, and he headed back to the fire. He was still hungry and wanted more coffee. He was relieved when he saw that Father Lambert was no longer there. He was in no mood for arguing with the priest about his partaking in something so natural as sex with a willing and eager Indian woman.

"Well, Black Buffalo," Barlow said as he sat and poured himself some coffee, "when're you fixin' to leave to go look for them Small Robes?"

"Right away. Tell me more about your Anna first. Then I go," the Flathead said quietly.

"She'd be five winters now. Fairly light skin, but she could be mistook for an Injin, I reckon. Dark eyes, like her ma's people, but her hair's more curly than you'd find in a Chinook, and not so black in color. She was chubby and healthy and full of laughin' when last I saw her."

Black Buffalo nodded solemnly. "I'll do what I can to see if we find her."

"I'd be powerfully obliged," Barlow said, trying to fight back the sudden surge of hope in his heart.

The Flathead rose and spoke briefly in his own language to Bull Heart and then went to where the women were gathered. Raising the Lodge stood and walked off toward the small herd of ponies. Black Buffalo talked to the women for a few moments, too. Soon after he had finished, Raising the Lodge returned with his pony ready for him to ride. Slow Sun hurried off and swiftly came back with his shield, quiver, and old musket. Black Buffalo took the weapons and swung onto the horse. For the first time since Barlow had met Black Buffalo, the warrior looked like a warrior, sitting tall and proud on the pony. He swung the horse's head around and moved out, the quiver on his back swaying with the animal's rhythmic walk.

When Black Buffalo had ridden out of sight into the trees, Barlow looked at White Bear. "Reckon we best go make some meat, hoss."

"You and Bull Heart go make meat, old chap," White

Bear said with a slight grin. "I have some things that need seein' to right here." He glanced over at Far Thunder, who was looking at him. She smiled a little and quickly turned away.

Barlow had followed White Bear's look and grinned widely. "Need to—how'd you say it?—put old Nebuchadnezzar out to grass? That it, ol' hoss?"

"Exactly right, mate," White Bear said, laughing. "I figure I can use the time you're away to talk some sense into that lass."

"Reckon you can, too, you sweet-tongued red devil," Barlow said with a laugh. He looked at the Flathead youth. "You up for some more huntin', hoss?" he asked.

Bull Heart grinned and nodded. "Huntin' good."

"That it is, boy," Barlow said with a nod. "And you're damn good at it, too. Go on and saddle up ol' Beelzebub for me. I'll be along directly."

The youth nodded and trotted off.

"You sure you're gonna be all right here by yourself, hoss?" Barlow asked.

White Bear nodded. "I think so. I don't expect any bloomin' Blackfeet to come skulkin' around. And there ain't no one else to be concerned with."

"What about the priest?" Barlow asked with a laugh. "He's gonna be powerful put out if you start beddin' Far Thunder out here in the full light of day."

"Perhaps he'll keep to his own bloody self, old chap. Else I'll treat that glocky choker to a do down he'll never forget." White Bear half laughed and half scowled.

"I reckon that all means something," Barlow said with a grin.

"Aye. It means I'll whale the tar out of that half-witted clergyman until he's within an inch of passin' on."

"Jist make certain you keep your eyes open whilst you're havin' your way with that innocent little gal."

"Innocent? Like hell, mate. I reckon she's dabbed it up good with a mess of other blokes long before this old chap came along." He grinned.

"You're probably right about that, hoss." Barlow pushed himself up. "Well, you have yourself a shinin' time whilst me and the boy are out takin' care of business." He smiled and winked.

"I aim to." White Bear returned the grin and wink.

Barlow and Buffalo headed off. Bull Heart had Beelzebub saddled and his own pony ready to go. They mounted up and Barlow led the way out of camp. Soon after, Bull Heart, who towed two pack mules behind him, pulled up alongside Barlow. "We hunt buffalo today?" he asked hopefully.

"That what you want, boy?"

Bull Heart nodded and grinned. "Buffler best. It shines, dammit."

Barlow laughed. "That it does, hoss. That it does. All right, so we'll go chase us down some buffler and have us some fine eatin' this night."

They picked up the pace, knowing they had a ride of several miles before the would find any buffalo. They finally spotted a small herd just after midday. Within minutes, they had run down two big cows and set about butchering the animals. As usual, they took only the finest cuts, leaving the rest where it lay. They rode slowly back, the pack mules laden down with bundles of buffalo meat dripping from bloody hunks of hide.

The two got back to camp late in the afternoon. The women hurried over and took the pack mules. In short order, meat was cooking at both fires. By the time Barlow and Bull Heart had taken care of the animals, it was time to eat. Barlow and Bull Heart sat at the fire with White Bear, who looked like a cat who just ate a mouse.

"Reckon you had a pleasurable day, hoss," Barlow said with a grin.

"Aye, mate!"

"That shines." Barlow's grin widened. "But tomorrow, you can go out and make meat."

"I believe that's only fair," White Bear responded sourly. Then he chuckled.

They were served by Raven Moon, Far Thunder, and Raising the Lodge. Midway through the meal, a sullen Father Lambert arrived and sat at the fire. He said nothing to the others, but it was obvious he was incensed. It was also quite clear what he was furious about. He glowered at White Bear, as if calling upon God to visit lightning on the Shoshoni right this instant. That such a thing did not happen only angered the priest all the more.

After eating, Lambert repaired to his tent right away. The others, who sat there sipping coffee, puffing pipes, and talking quietly, soon heard Lambert reciting the Rosary and then later praying. Barlow considered yelling at the priest to shut up, but he decided that this way at least they knew where he was and what he was doing, rather than perhaps bringing him back out ranting and raving against their impious ways.

They turned in soon after dark, Raven Moon accompanying Barlow and Far Thunder escorting White Bear to their bedrolls.

As they lay there catching their breath after making love, Barlow pulled Raven Moon close. "You sure this is all right?" he asked.

"Yes. Very good!" Raven Moon responded enthusiastically.

Barlow grinned. "I meant that you're leavin' your daughter each night. Won't Yellow Leaf wonder where you've gotten yourself off to?"

Raven Moon cuddled a little closer, comfortable in

the big, powerful cocoon Barlow provided. "She asleep already when I come with you. If she wakes, Little Star Woman or one of the others care for her. If she ask where I am, they tell her I'm with you."

"And that's all right?"

"Yes. Very."

Barlow nodded into the night. "Yellow Leaf sure is a purty little thing," he said quietly, his voice catching at the remembrance of his own daughter. "She reminds me an awful lot of my Anna."

"Is that good?" Raven Moon asked, suddenly worried.

Barlow was silent for some time as he thought that one over. "I reckon it is," he finally said. "It's hurtful in some ways to see a little gal like that who reminds me so much of Anna. But at the same time, it's pleasant to have a young'n like that around *to* remind me of Anna. It keeps me filled with hope that I'll find my chil' one day before much longer."

"Then it is good," Raven Moon said firmly. She yawned and wriggled a little against him, enjoying the feel of his hard muscular body against her flesh. In moments she was asleep, her head resting on his shoulder and upper chest.

Sleep was not as easy in coming for Barlow. His thoughts had turned to Anna. He wondered how long it would be before Black Buffalo returned—and whether he would have any useful information. Doubt began to flood over Barlow again. At such times, he was sure he would never be able to track Anna down. The thought made his heart and soul shrink into a small black knot that festered inside and ate away at him. And it seemed to him that each time it happened, it got just a little more difficult to overcome the bleakness and restore his normal humors.

• • •

The next two days were much the same as the previous one. Barlow and White Bear took turns hunting with Bull Heart and staying behind with the women. About the only real difference was that on the second morning, Father Lambert came out of his tent in fine fettle. He roared and ranted at both Barlow and White Bear, cursed them as fornicators and spawn of the devil himself. He screeched and thundered and yelled. Trouble was, after the first couple of minutes, most of what he spouted was in French. While Barlow and White Bear might be able to follow a few phrases or words in that language, they were hopeless beyond that, and so didn't really understand more than a word here and there that Lambert said.

Not that they needed to be fluent in French to get the drift of Lambert's thundering sermon of fire and brimstone. During the first few minutes, when he was still speaking what passed for English, they had gotten the picture. They figured that all the rest was more along the same lines. So they stoically sat through his ranting sermon—for a while.

After nearly half an hour on continuous invective from the rampaging priest, both subjects had had their fill of it.

As Lambert paused to suck in a chestful of air before launching into his rant again, White Bear shouted, "Get knotted, you bloody annoying bastard."

"*Quell*?" Lambert asked. "What did you say to me, monsieur?" His face was bright red with choler.

"I said, old chap—shut up! You're enough to make a man go on the bleedin' war path."

"I got to agree with White Bear, hoss," Barlow offered. He was angry at the berating he had just undergone but was trying to keep a cap on his temper. "You are sure one vexatious goddamn critter."

Lambert was dumbstruck for some seconds but then

launched into another tirade, this time in French right from the start.

This time Barlow let it go on only a few seconds before he pushed himself off the stump on which he was sitting and roared, "Shut your yammerin' trap, you irritating son of a bitch!" His anger made him seem even larger than he was.

Lambert plopped down on the rock he had often used as a seat and cowered under Barlow's harsh glare and threatening bulk.

"I've had jist about enough of your sanctimonious blather," Barlow bellowed.

"As have I, old chap," White Bear snapped, moving up to stand beside Barlow.

These twin towers of belligerence frightened Lambert all the more, and he cringed.

"And if you keep this foolishness up, you bloody dumb bastard, I'll nobble you but good."

Barlow glanced quizzically at his Shoshoni friend.

"I'll inflict grievous bodily harm on that bleedin', self-righteous bugger," Barlow interpreted.

Barlow nodded. "And I'll help him, hoss," he tossed in. He paused. "Now go on back to your tent, damn you, and leave us be. Pray for our souls, if you feel you have to, but keep yourself out of our doin's."

Frightened, Lambert stood and scuttled backward toward his tent, almost tripping several times on rocks and roots. He finally turned and scurried into his tent.

Barlow and White Bear watched him, then sat, still angry. A few minutes later, they looked at each other. Each grinned, then more widely, and then they laughed loud and raucously.

11

LATE IN THE afternoon of the third day since leaving, Black Buffalo rode back into the camp. With him were two hard-looking Indians whom Barlow assumed were Small Robes.

With little preamble, the men took their places around the fire. All except Father Lambert, who remained in his tent, praying loudly, beseeching God to deliver him from such heathens as Barlow and White Bear.

Some of the women took the warriors' ponies away to tend to them, while most of the others hurriedly served up food—hunks of fresh buffalo brought in just hours before, and stew made of buffalo simmered with roots and herbs. And coffee.

When the men had eaten, Black Buffalo pulled out his ceremonial pipe and lit the long calumet with Bull Heart's assistance. Black Buffalo puffed a moment to make sure it was going properly. He blew smoke in the four cardinal directions, then toward the ground and the sky. He passed it to the Small Robe who was sitting on his right. That Indian went through the ritual before passing it to his companion. The pipe made its way around the circle of men until it was back to Black Buffalo, who set it aside. Then he nodded.

One of the Small Robes—Four Dogs—spoke, using his own language, which was translated into English by Black Buffalo.

"The Hudson's Bay Company has been tryin' to deal with various Blackfoot bands for some years now," Four Dogs said through Black Buffalo. "That's why one of the company's men from Fort Hall went with the men you said had taken Anna from White Bear."

"That was Finan McTavish's man, Aaron Dunne?" Barlow asked.

Four Dogs nodded.

"And he was to talk with the Blackfeet for Bob Carruthers and his goddamn friends?"

Four Dogs nodded again, once Black Buffalo had translated for him. "Yes," he said as Black Buffalo continued translating, "he talk for other white-eyes. The ones who bring children with them. They parley long and hard, but things look good, all goin' well, until the white-eyes—except for Hudson's Bay Company man—got greedy. They want too much. They ask for more and more. The Blackfoot get angry then. White-eyes get angry, too."

"Goddamn idiots," Barlow muttered. "Nary satisfied. Fractious, stupid bastards."

"Calm down, old chap," White Bear said quietly. "They've paid the price for their glocky behavior."

Barlow nodded, not assuaged very much.

"That's when the Blackfeet attack the white-eyes," Four Dogs added, still speaking through Black Buffalo. "And the other two who came then." Four Dogs smiled a little, indicating that while he and his band, though related to the Blackfeet, had no love for their cousins.

"That'd be me and White Bear, wouldn't it?" Barlow asked harshly.

"Yes," Four Dogs answered through Black Buffalo. "You drive off the Blackfeet, but they had the children already, taken from the white-eyes they had killed. They keep the children over the winter. In the spring, a group of warriors headed north and east with some of the children. They planned to give them to other bands."

"Why?" Barlow asked, surprised.

"Many Blackfeet have died from the white-eyes sicknesses. Many, many. The children from other tribes will help to replace some of the children lost in the spotted sickness."

"But haven't the band who has the young'uns lost children, too?" Barlow asked.

"Yes, of course. They planned to keep some of the children themselves. But other bands have suffered much larger losses, and they will try to help those bands." Four Dogs paused, then added, "It's thought that many of the Blackfeet bands will go on the war path and seek to capture other children to restore their ranks."

Barlow nodded. It all made some sense. Smallpox, and to a lesser extent cholera, had decimated some of the Blackfeet bands. To increase their raids to capture children to replace some of those lost to disease was to be expected. And to divide up the children they already had made sense, too. "Was my Anna amongst those taken north?" he asked nervously.

"I think so," Four Dogs said with a firm nod.

"Where was they headin'?" Barlow asked.

"To some bands on the Musselshell and along the Milk River, as the white-eyes called it," Black Buffalo translated.

Barlow glanced at White Bear, who stared blankly back at him. Finally, Barlow looked at Black Buffalo.

"I reckon that's where I'll be headin', too, hoss," he said evenly.

"That's not what we agreed on, my friend," Black Buffalo responded simply, evenly.

Barlow shrugged. "No matter now, hoss. Me'n White Bear will be headin' for the Musselshell country come first light."

"We had deal," Black Buffalo argued. "I keep my part. Now you go back on yours?"

Barlow nodded. "A man's got to do what he feels is necessary when the time comes, hoss," he said without remorse. "Savin' my Anna's a hell of a lot more important that helpin' you and your people git back to your homeland."

"Then you're no better than Black Robe Lambert. You say one thing to get what you seek, then say another when that suits you. Like many white-eyes, you speak with the forked tongue of the serpent."

"Now hold on a minute there, hoss," Barlow snapped, his anger growing even greater. "Don't you go callin' this ol' chil' no forked tongue ol' hoss. It jist ain't true."

"But you not keep your word," Black Buffalo said evenly.

"Well, I meant to. But with this new information I got, you cain't hold me to what I promised the other day."

"Why not?"

"Because things're different now, hoss. What these boys"—he indicated the two Small Robes—"have told me makes me need to git on with things and go find my daughter."

"So you take back your word to me, to my people," Black Buffalo responded simply. "That is not—"

"Stop arguing with 'im, Monsieur Black Buffalo," Lambert said. He had walked up quietly, unnoticed, and was standing about ten feet behind the Flathead war leader. "It is 'opeless. 'E will not listen. 'E 'as made up 'is mind, and 'is promises of old mean nothing. It is another sign of 'is sinful ways. Ze Lord punishes liars, Monsieur Barlow. And you 'ave many sins you will 'ave to answer for when Judgment Day comes, monsieur."

"Go to hell, hoss," Barlow growled. He was in no mood for the priest's moralizing.

"The Black Robe speaks true this time, Barlow," Black Buffalo said, dark eyes glittering with his own rising anger.

"He's spoutin' off buffler shit, and you damn well know it, hoss," Barlow snapped. "He's jist tryin' to turn you against me."

"I don't need the Black Robe's words to turn me against you right now. Your words do that." Black Buffalo's face hardened.

Barlow shook his head, his anger and irritation not letting him think or see clearly. All he wanted right now was to head off after Anna before something else happened to her. He could not understand why Black Buffalo and the others could not realize that. "I got to save Anna," he said stubbornly. "I ain't sure why, but it seems important as all hell to try'n get her afore them bastards wind up takin' her to the Canada lands."

"It's too late for that, old chap," White Bear said quietly. "If they were on the trail in the spring, she's wherever she's gonna be up thataway, and if some band drifts in to Canada, there's ain't no stoppin' it."

"But if they take her to Canada, I ain't ary gonna git her back," Barlow half-whined.

"That's a glocky—half-witted—notion, mate, and you know it," White Bear said evenly.

"You turnin' against me too, ol' hoss?" Barlow demanded, turning his harsh glare on the Shoshoni.

"You're daft, you bloody damn fool. Use your head, mate."

"I am, goddammit!"

"Like hell. Your mind's set on one thing, old chap, and you can't see anything different because of that. Now, I know you're a man who's never gone back on his word. You're not a gammy—false—type of bloke. And now's not the time to change your ways."

Barlow hesitated before saying anything, and White Bear jumped into the breach again. "Besides, Canada ain't no trouble, far's I can tell. You can't even tell where one bloody country ends and the other begins." He smiled a bit harshly. "Besides, mate, the Hudson's Bay Company holds sway over all of bloomin' Canada from what I heard."

"So?"

"So, if she's there, your chances of gettin' her back are better than ever, since the bloody Company will probably help."

Barlow stewed over that for a while, shaking his head the whole time. Every fiber of his being called for him to saddle up Beelzebub and ride out of here right now, despite night being almost on them. But what White Bear had said to him was true. He was not a man to go back on his word. He was in a hell of a bind, and he wasn't comfortable with that. He wanted to go for Anna, but at the same time, his conscience would not let him easily go back on his word.

"You know, Barlow," Black Buffalo said quietly, "my people will not make it back to our homeland alone. We need your help—and your protection—to be safe on the journey. That's what you promised to do."

"I know that's what I said I'd do, hoss," Barlow snapped, more annoyed by the fact that Black Buffalo was right. He poured himself some more coffee and tore off a chunk of buffalo meat. He chewed the meat slowly, trying to settle himself down some. He hoped that by doing so he might be able to get Blackfoot to see it his way, or at least explain himself better.

After several minutes, Barlow said, "Get the Small Robes to go with you, Black Buffalo. They're friends with your people and should be pleased to do you such a kindness."

Black Buffalo talked with Four Dogs and Big Eagle for some minutes. Barlow could understand nothing of the conversation. Then the Flathead leader looked back at Barlow. "The Small Robes can't help," he said. "They must get back to their own people. They fear the Blackfeet will come against them again for helpin' us—and to finish fight they start last time."

"You sure they're tellin' true?" Barlow asked roughly. "You sure they jist ain't sayin' that 'cause they feel like goin' home?"

"Knowin' much about the other Blackfeet bands, I think the Small Robes speak true," Black Buffalo responded, trying to keep his rising anger in check. "I think Blackfeet will attack the Small Robes again." He paused. "And I think Blackfeet will attack us again as we make our way back to our land."

Still angry, and growing angrier at the probable loss of this whole argument, Barlow looked at White Bear. "You think Black Buffalo here's tellin' true, too?"

"Why wouldn't he, old chap?"

"Who knows what they were yappin' about in their own tongues," Barlow said thoughtfully. "They might've been discussin' the last ceremony they had together, and then let me and you think they were talkin' over the Small Robes' inability to help their friends."

"You have a delightfully demented mind, old chap," White Bear said. He was almost slightly amused.

"That right?"

White Bear nodded. "Do you really think Black Buffalo would go through all that trouble just to fool you, mate?"

"Damn," Barlow spit out. He felt a complete fool for his unfounded—and ridiculous, once he thought about it—ideas. But his mind was really on Anna. He could not stand the fact that he seemingly got caught in these quandaries all the time, continually having to postpone his search for Anna.

Barlow rose and stomped off, as much to let his anger cool as to give himself time to think. He wandered down toward the river. He sat on a rock, angrily pitching stones into the water. He sat there until it was almost dark, then he rose, his mind made up, and headed back toward the fire.

He took his former seat and poured some more coffee. He sipped some, knowing he was irritating the others, but not really caring right then. Finally, he set the tin mug down and looked at Black Buffalo. "Sorry, ol' hoss," he said quietly, "but I've got my Anna to think of first. I've come close to findin' her so many times, and always have been a little too late to save her. Well, by God, I ain't gonna let that happen again."

Barlow turned his steady gaze to White Bear. "We been through a heap of hard times, ol' hoss," he said, still speaking civilly. "And some good ones, too." He conjured up a sudden vision of he and White Bear each making love to two sisters they had encountered on a wagon train the previous summer. "But I can understand if you think what I'm doin' is wrong. I told you a long time ago, my friend, that this really ain't none of your doin's. I'm obliged you've ridden the trail with me for so long. But if you figure you need to stay with the Flatheads here and help 'em git home, then that's what you should do. But I got to git on the trail of my Anna."

Barlow sighed and looked back at Black Buffalo. "It don't shine with this chil' none to go back on his word, hoss," he said somewhat apologetically. "But findin' Anna's most important to me right now. I reckon you don't like that, but I hope that, since you've jist lost a son, that you can understand." He looked hopeful.

"I understand," Black Buffalo said, though his expression belied his words. His shoulders seemed to slump a little. "It will be as you say."

"Now, hold on here, old chap," White Bear interjected. "There's one big thing you seem to be forgetting, friend Will."

"And what's that?" Barlow asked, not really caring.

White Bear pointed toward the other fire.

Barlow shrugged. "Raven Moon's a fine woman, and the time she'n I've spent together has been shinin'. But she ain't worth leavin' my Anna out there a moment longer than I have to."

"I'm not talkin' about Raven Moon, old chap," Barlow said in disdain. "Look at those little ones over there. The little ones."

Barlow turned, knowing even before he did that he had lost this battle pure and simple. Seeing the faces of the youngsters—especially Yellow Leaf—Barlow knew he could not allow himself to be responsible for the death of these young children. He cursed silently at this latest obstacle to finding Anna, but he knew he had no choice now. He turned back to face Black Buffalo. "I will go with you as I promised," he said as a sick feeling crawled up his stomach and lodged in his throat.

12

THEY PULLED OUT the next morning. The two sullen Short Robes headed mostly east and a little north, almost immediately fading into the mist that swirled around the river. Barlow wondered about the two more than a little. There seemed to be something about them that prickled the hair on the back of his neck. There was nothing immediate that he could put a finger on, but they left him unsettled. He had given considerable thought to Four Dogs and Big Eagle during the night—before Raven Moon had delightfully distracted him—and had concluded they were not to be trusted. What that would mean, he wasn't sure, but he more than half suspected he would run into them again, and when he did, he would not be as trusting of them as Black Buffalo seemed to be.

Barlow's group went almost due west. White Bear and Black Buffalo led the procession, riding together on the trail that wove through the trees along the banks of the river. Later, as the trail widened, they would spread out a little more, increasing the range of their watchfulness, while never really getting out of sight of the others. The women and children—and Father Lambert—followed, along with the pack animals and extra ponies. Some of the women herded the animals, while the others kept an eye on the children. Barlow and Bull Heart brought up the rear, making sure no one lagged and keeping an eye out for any potential enemies who might follow. Buffalo 2 made his own trail, but usually did not stray too far from Barlow.

They rode steadily though not hurriedly, taking it easy on the animals and themselves. If the Blackfeet did decide to come after them, they wanted to be as fresh as possible for the battle. During the afternoon, Bull Heart cut out two pack animals and veered off, heading into the forest. He returned with an elk and a deer carcass on the pack mules. They would feed well tonight.

The day passed in uneventful monotony, and before dark Black Buffalo directed them to a quiet spot amid the trees along a swift little brook. Wood, water, and forage were all plentiful. With a storm threatening, the women put up two lodges—one to be shared by Barlow, Raven Moon, White Bear, and Far Thunder and the other for the rest of the Flatheads—and Lambert's tent. A light rain started as the camp went up, but the people were warm and dry before the precipitation really let loose.

The meat was distributed, as was a supply of coffee and sugar. One of Black Buffalo's old wives took care of serving Lambert. Raven Moon and Far Thunder cooked for Barlow, White Bear, and Yellow Leaf. There was less formality now that they were under cover, and the women often laughed as they worked.

With the growing darkness, the wind picked up and the temperature dropped. The rain fell steadily and hard, punctuated by bursts of driven rain. Adding to the atmosphere was the sharp, sizzling shards of lightning and the foreboding rumble of thunder.

As the two men waited for their food, Barlow asked, "What do you think of them Small Robes?"

"Four Dogs and Big Eagle, old chap? Or all of 'em?"

"Our two recent guests," Barlow said flatly.

White Bear shrugged. "I wasn't too impressed with them, mate," he offered as he stretched out his legs.

"You trust 'em? Or what they say?" Barlow asked anxiously. He listened to the thunder and the pounding of the rain on the skin lodge, and was grateful he was not out in the midst of the storm. He wondered, though, where Anna was, and whether it was storming where she was.

White Bear pondered his response for a considerable time before he shook his head. "Can't say as I do, old chap. Hadn't really thought of it before, but now that I do, I'd say I wouldn't wager a pence on what they had to say."

"That's what I were thinkin', too." Barlow was agitated. He was certain now that the Small Robes had lied to him. But to what avail? And what did it mean to him now? Only more searching, really, though he hated that he might be sent in the wrong direction by their lies.

"Try to put it out of mind, old chap," White Bear said quietly. "As soon as we get the Flatheads back to their homeland, we'll get us back here and find your Anna. We're no worse off than we were before."

"Reckon you're right," Barlow responded skeptically. He was still tortured by the thoughts brought on by the possibility that the Small Robes were lying.

"Maybe one of the first stops we can make is among the Small Robes and have a little chat with Four Dogs and Big Eagle."

Barlow nodded. That would be something to hold on

to until he could return here and continue his quest. Finding the two warriors might be a lot easier than finding Anna, and once he did, he vowed that he would make them talk—and tell the truth this time. He tried without success to banish the thought that they might actually know nothing about Anna's whereabouts. If that were the case, however, Barlow promised himself that they would pay the highest price for the lies they had already told.

Food was soon ready, and they all ate. An evening of lovemaking in the robes with the delectable Raven Moon helped Barlow keep the Small Robes from his mind for a while, especially when he became aware of White Bear and Far Thunder engaging in their own bouts of intercourse, and the two men, as they had been known to do before, made a contest of their carnal enjoyments. Nothing was really said directly, but their grunts and groans and heaving, as well as the gasps of excitement the men elicited from the women, all served as challenges, victory cheers, and—to some extent—as catcalls to the other.

Sated, sleep came easily.

The rain was still teeming in the morning, and the men gathered in Black Buffalo's lodge to discuss the day's travel. The Flathead leader—acknowledging the arguments his two wives had made before they had all arisen for the morning—decided that they would stay the day here. They had plenty of fresh meat yet, plus wood. The animals had plenty of forage, and the travelers were in no big hurry.

Barlow chafed a bit at the decision but decided it was not worth arguing about. He had done more than his share of traveling in the rain—and in the inevitable mud and muck it stirred up—that he had no great desire to do so again. Better to stay warm and dry and comfortable, spend the day in carnal pursuits, and make up some distance tomorrow than try to travel in the rain at the risk of losing an animal from a leg breaking in the slop. They could easily make up in the next day or two what mileage they might splash through today.

So Barlow and White Bear, accompanied by their women, returned to their lodge to renew their profligate competition, much to the delight of Raven Moon and Far Thunder, who had decided to hold their own little tournament.

They pulled out the next morning with somewhat renewed spirits. The rained continued, but it had slackened considerably, and the sky off in the distance showed evidence that the storm would have passed by before the sun reached its zenith.

The going was slow that day with the ground slick with mud spawned by the rain. It made for some treacherous going up the hills and steeper mountains trails, but they took their time. By midafternoon, the rain had stopped, and the sun returned with brutal force.

No lodges went up that night, and Black Buffalo decided that even Father Lambert would do without his tent. The priest protested, but the Flathead leader ignored him. Finally, Lambert went to Barlow.

"Monsieur Barlow," he said plaintively, "will you 'elp me reason with zis savage? 'E 'as—"

"He's plenty reasonable, hoss," Barlow replied crossly. "Ain't none of the rest of us need a lodge. Cain't see why you'd need one."

"I should 'ave known you would be zis way," Lambert complained. "You are as bad as zese savages."

"You keep tellin' me so," Barlow responded with an insolent grin. "Mayhap you're right. 'Course it don't make me no nevermind just what you think, hoss." He went back to unloading one of the mules.

In a snit, the priest spun and stalked off, the bottom of his cassock swirling.

Without the need to take down lodges and such, they were able to leave a bit earlier the next morning, and they pushed on through the increasingly bright and hot sunshine. The ground was drying rapidly under the sun's assault, and the group picked up the pace, making up most of the time they had lost to the storm two days ago.

The next few days were much the same. The travelers moved steadily through the hot days and made minimal camps at night. The monotony was as dull and wearing as the sun was bright. Despite the heat, however, everyone except the priest could feel the touch of fall that seemed to be lurking right behind the great solar ball. As soon as the sun went down these days, the temperatures would drop. Because of it, Barlow was mighty grateful to have Raven Moon in his sleeping robes at night. She was like his own little hearth in the robes— hot and fiery—and she kept him plenty warm in the night's chill.

Along with the certainty that fall was soon to arrive, Barlow began to feel a sureness that the travelers were being watched or followed. More than once over the next couple of days, he wheeled Beelzebub away from the group for a spell, riding up into the trees, or climbing a hillside, where he would plant himself for a while and patiently wait and keep a vigil. But he saw nothing out of the ordinary.

He kept silent about it for two days, but that night, as he and White Bear were eating, and their women had gone off to join their friends for a bit, Barlow told the Shoshoni of his feelings.

"But you've not seen anyone, old chap?" White Bear questioned.

Barlow shook his head, annoyed at the situation, and angry at himself for not being able to resolve it somehow.

"But you know someone's out there?"

"Yep, goddammit," Barlow hissed.

"Any notion of who it might be?" White Bear trusted in Barlow's instincts, and he was quite familiar with the feeling that Barlow was experiencing. It was a prickly feeling on the back of his neck, the absolute assurance that someone was there—somewhere—despite any real evidence of it.

Barlow gave him a baleful look.

"Blackfeet, you think, eh, old chap?"

"Who else," Barlow responded, making it a statement, not a question. "But if those bastards're there, they're sure makin' themselves mighty goddamn hard to see."

"Not unusual for bloody Blackfeet," White Bear said with a small smile.

"Well, I reckon that's a goddamn fact." Barlow paused. "You don't think I've gone mad, do you, White Bear?" he suddenly asked. "Mayhap because I've been thinkin' so much about Anna bein' in the hands of those red devils that I've lost my reason and am startin' to think there's Blackfeet where there really ain't any?"

"No, my friend, I don't think you're daft," White Bear responded quietly. "Far from it. We both know those Blackfeet're gonna come against us sooner or later. I think maybe you're just pickin' up sign a mite early is all, old chap. Sort of anticipatin' things."

Barlow sighed and rubbed a callused hand over his weary face. "I sure hope you're right, hoss," he said. "I got enough real concerns plaguin' me without conjurin' up ones that ain't real."

"Those bloody Blackfeet will show you they're for real soon enough, old chap."

"I reckon they will," Barlow responded, reassured.

"I think we should let Black Buffalo and Bull Heart know, even though we have no evidence of any bloomin' Blackfeet bein' nearby just yet. They might be extra wary whilst they're out huntin' or even while just ridin' along with us."

Barlow nodded. "I'll tell 'em both before we leave in the mornin'. Now I reckon it's time for this ol' chil' to fill his meatbag."

"A fine thought, old chap," White Bear agreed.

They ate well on the ducks that Bull Heart had brought down during the day, and they soon turned in, using their sleeping robes but not lodges.

The next morning, as they were preparing to leave, Barlow paid a visit to Black Buffalo, who, as usual, was doing nothing about breaking camp. Such work was beneath his dignity as a warrior. The warrior was sitting with young Bull Heart, who also did little in the way of making or breaking camp. Despite his age, he, too, was a Flathead warrior, so was not expected to take part in such menial tasks.

Barlow explained his feelings and suggested that Black Buffalo and Bull Heart be extra vigilant. He was glad that neither Indian thought his reasons unusual. Both simply accepted his statements, and his rationale, at face value and promised to watch more closely as they rode.

They moved out soon after, Barlow still feeling uneasy, even more so now that he had brought the subject out into the open. He almost hoped that Blackfeet would pop up, just to prove to himself that his instincts were correct.

No enemy Indians presented themselves that day, however. Still, no one made light of Barlow's concerns. Of the warriors, only Bull Heart had not really experienced such a feeling before, and they knew the uncertainty that came with it.

Barlow's feeling that they were being followed and watched grew stronger as the next day progressed. Finally, right about midday, Barlow pulled off the trail after a word with Bull Heart, and he moved at a right angle to the group. He rode slowly, senses alert, Buffalo 2 trotting around him. He heard nothing unusual—simply the natural sounds to be expected, the birds, a hawk circling above emitting its high-pitched shriek, some geese honking.

Suddenly Buffalo stopped, head up, ears pointed, nose working. Barlow pulled to a halt and listened intently. He heard nothing out of the ordinary, but he knew something was not right by the way Buffalo was acting. He maneuvered Beelzebub into some thick brush and sat, waiting. Buffalo stood next to the mule, nose working, almost vibrating as he sought out the foreign smells.

Then Barlow heard a quickly stifled horse neighing. It came from a direction far removed from where his fellow travelers were. Moments later he heard the soft clomp of unshod hooves. He needed no other proof. Tapping his leg to get Beelzebub to move, he eased the big mule out of the brush, turned it toward the column of travelers, and moved on, slowly at first, so as not to attract attention, but then more swiftly as he made his way away from the presumed enemy closing in on them.

13

BARLOW HIT A meadow and kicked Beelzebub into a run, heading at an angle to where his group would soon be moving. Through more trees and out onto a mostly flat little glade again, he rode hard. Within minutes he spotted his traveling companions. He did not slow as he splattered across an extremely shallow, eight-foot-wide, rocky-bottomed stream and quickly gained on the others.

White Bear must have heard or sensed something, as he, being the nearer of he and Black Buffalo, who were at the head of the small column, turned and saw him. White Bear shouted something and the travelers slowly ground to a halt and turned to wait for his arrival.

Barlow pulled up his blowing mule. "Blackfeet're comin'," he said without preliminary. "Ain't sure how many."

"They comin' for us, old chap?" White Bear asked.

"Well, I nary stopped to ask 'em, hoss," Barlow responded with some sarcasm, "but I'd reckon so."

White Bear nodded. "Just making sure, mate." He

paused. "So, old chap, do you have any idea of what to do?"

"Jist hold up, hoss," Barlow said. He took nearly a full minute to survey the landscape, but there was no real good place to make a stand. He finally pointed his rifle. About half a mile ahead, across the glade along the meandering stream, was a line of trees as far as the eye could see. To the southwest, it was a thin line, barely a few trees deep, but it widened considerably on the northeast as it rose onto a small, grassy hill. The trees covered the top of the hillock and appeared to run off into the distance beyond and to the northwest.

"I reckon that's the best we can do," Barlow said. "If our medicine shines, those boys'll pass by without bein' none the wiser about us."

"Let them come," Bull Heart said, his young warrior's face arrogant and determined. "I'm not afraid of the Blackfeet."

"Then you ain't got the sense God give a rock, boy," Barlow snapped. In a way, he understood the youth's desire to fight. He would favor that himself, believing that to get it over with would be better. But since they had no idea how many Blackfeet they would be facing, hoping to skip a battle now was wisest especially when their cover was rather limited. On the other hand, without a fight now, they would have to be ever-more vigilant, since the Blackfeet would be in close proximity and would be bound to pick up on their trail soon. Playing hide-and-seek with the Blackfeet between here and the Flatheads' home village would likely be deadly.

"Let's move," Black Buffalo ordered. He headed off at a good pace, taking Bull Heart with him this time. Barlow and White Bear waited until the others had gone past and were some yards ahead, then swung in behind them and followed slowly, keeping a watch on the trail behind them.

Black Buffalo and Bull Heart were first at the small hill and immediately began directing the women to where the horses and mules should be held. By the time Barlow, White Bear, and Buffalo arrived, the animals—except the ones still being ridden by the two Flathead warriors, the Shoshoni, and the white man—were ensconced deep in the trees, where they would be relatively safe. The four fighting men sat on the slope of the hill, unafraid of being seen from the flats because of the hill and the trees behind them, and watched.

Though time dragged on, no one said anything. No one questioned Barlow's original warning. All knew the white man well enough to be pretty certain he had seen what he had said he had seen. It was quite possible that the Blackfeet had been moving in a slightly different direction and would not come too close to their position.

Eventually, though, Black Buffalo pointed. "There," he said simply.

To their left, perhaps half a mile away, was a line of Blackfeet warriors. They moved slowly along at a slight angle that would bring them just to the right of the small hill on which Barlow and his friends stood. There was no chance they would be missed, unless the Blackfeet veered off soon. They showed no sign of doing so, however.

Bull Heart sidled his pony up alongside Barlow, who was sitting on Beelzebub. "Why don't you and me take the battle to 'em before they get here?" the young Flathead suggested.

"Too foolish, boy," Barlow said flatly.

"You afraid?" Bull Heart challenged.

"Of what? Blackfeet?" Barlow snorted. "Ain't ary

been a day for sich. But these doins take some sense, hoss."

"What's that mean?"

"It means, boy, that we don't know how many of them critters're out there. It means that if we go on out there and suddenly we're facin' half the goddamn Blackfoot nation, that we're gonna go under. Now that may not bother you none, boy, but it don't suit this chil' to git his ass rubbed out for no sound reason. And if we was to git turned into worm food out there, there's only be Black Buffalo and White Bear to protect all the woman and children and sich."

"You are too headstrong, Bull Heart," Black Buffalo said in Flathead. A smile almost cracked his stern visage. "That's not always a bad thing, but it must be tempered." In English he added, "You listen to Barlow. He a smart man about these things."

Barlow did not respond to the compliment, though he was pleased. He watched a little longer, and when it became apparent that the Blackfeet would not bypass this small hill, he dismounted, and waved at Raven Moon. When the woman appeared at his side, he handed her the reins to the mule, then took his looking glass from a bag hanging from the saddle. "Keep him safe, but make sure he's close by," Barlow ordered softly. "And leave him saddled."

Raven Moon nodded. As she began to lead Beelzebub away, she also took the reins for Black Buffalo's pony. Far Thunder, who was only a moment behind Raven Moon coming out of the trees, took the horses from White Bear and Bull Heart and followed Raven Moon.

Barlow handed White Bear his telescope before kneeling in front of a fallen log and placing his shooting supplies and two single-shot belt pistols on it. Then he sprawled out on his belly, rifle resting on the log. He checked distance and the wind as best he could and made some estimates. Then he sat up, cross-legged, and waited some more.

The three other men sat, watching the Blackfeet's slow progression across the open land, its grass now brown, with the stream bisecting it. The war party seemed to be moving with incredible slowness, almost to the point that they were not moving at all. But they were and eventually the first few warriors were within a reasonable distance.

"Time to welcome these boys," Barlow said. He slid his legs out so that he was lying on his stomach again and sighted down the rifle. The others waited expectantly.

"Think you can hit anything from here, old chap?" White Bear asked casually.

"Ain't sure," Barlow responded sarcastically. "I had been thinkin' so, but with your stench affectin' my lead pill, I ain't positive no more."

Bull Heart listened to the exchange in astonishment, not realizing the two men were merely teasing each other. But he wisely kept his mouth closed.

White Bear and Black Buffalo watched the Blackfeet intently. The Shoshoni estimated that the distance to the lead Blackfoot was close to four hundred yards. He had seen Barlow make some fine shots, but nothing at this distance and, while he had a lot of faith in his friend's abilities, he was not sure about this.

Barlow fired. Before the powder smoke cleared from in front of his face, White Bear emitted a small shout, and Barlow knew he had hit his target. He set about reloading and then surveyed the field. Several Blackfeet were gathered around something in the grass—Barlow assumed it was the downed warrior. Others sat on their horses, looking around, trying to find out where the shot had come from.

Rifle reloaded, Barlow calmly fired again. One of the mounted Blackfeet toppled off his horse.

"*Mon dieu!*" Father Lambert muttered. He had finally come out of the trees and wandered down to where Barlow lay and the three warriors squatted. "Zat is some shooting, monsieur!"

Barlow ignored the priest and reloaded, then resettled himself. But there were no more targets. The Blackfeet had scattered their ponies and disappeared. Two riderless ponies wandered around looking nervous. He glanced over at White Bear, who had the telescope out and was studying the landscape through it.

"So, hoss?" Barlow asked. "What're them critters up to?"

"Lyin' low in the grass, old chap," White Bear responded, as if discussing the weather. "Hidin' like the bloody serpents they are."

"You count how many of 'em down there?"

"Thirteen—before you put those two in lavender."

"In lavender?" Barlow asked, giving the Shoshoni a questioning look.

"Put 'em under, old chap."

"So there's eleven of those bastards left?"

"From what I've seen, mate, yes." He sounded uncertain.

Barlow picked up on that. "Are you sure about that or not, hoss?" he asked.

"No, I'm not bloody sure," White Bear snapped. "That's all I see, but I have a hunch there's more of those bloomin' bastards about."

"Why's that?"

"I think I see movement back in the trees beyond them, old chap," White Bear said. He was annoyed that he could not be positive about any of this. "I think there's some others back in there that hadn't come out yet when you went off on your shootin' spree."

"That so?" Barlow said dryly. "I reckon you'd rather I had waited till them first ones was up here shakin' hands with us before firin' so's the ones in the woods there would've shown their faces?"

"Well, I don't expect I'd say that," White Bear protested. He pulled the glass away from his eye and sighed. "I just wish I could get a fix on those bleedin' bastards."

"Don't fret over it, hoss," Barlow said, sitting up. "They're nervous enough for the time bein' and will keep their heads down for at least a spell." He paused, thinking, then nodded. "Which means I think you and the others ought to git movin' again."

"To where?" White Bear asked, not surprised.

"On the trail toward Black Buffalo's village," Barlow said flatly. He glanced over at Black Buffalo. "You know of somewhere we might take cover for the night, a place that'd be easier to defend than this one, should that need arise?"

The Flathead leader nodded. "There's a good place half a day's ride." He pointed in a vaguely southwest direction.

"Can you make it before dark?"

Black Buffalo shook his head. "Don't think so. Not much later, though. But if we hurry, we can make it not too late."

"Then y'all best git on the move," Barlow ordered.

"What about you, old chap?" White Bear asked.

"I aim to set right here for a spell," Barlow responded. "I reckon I can discourage those goddamn critters down there from followin' us at least till dark falls."

"And then what?"

"Then I'll hightail it after all of you. Well, I reckon

I'll actually mosey along in the dark, and once light comes again, I can again offer those Blackfeet bastards some discouragement from continuin' to follow us. I'll catch up by tomorrow night, I expect."

"An excellent plan, monsieur," Lambert said hastily, his fear evident in his voice.

Everyone ignored him.

"I'll stay with you," Bull Heart volunteered, his voice firm.

"No, boy," Barlow said quietly. "I'm obliged by the offer, but the others'll need you more'n I will. You'll have your hands full tryin' to git all the women, children, and animals to safety. I'll have Buffler here with me and will be safe enough."

The others thought about that, before each man nodded.

"You need anything, old chap?" White Bear asked.

"Jist some meat and jerky. Maybe some water. Have Raven Moon tie Beelzebub over to yonder tree." He pointed to a solitary pine about ten yards away.

"You don't catch up to us by tomorrow night, old chap, I'm comin' after your bloody white ass," White Bear said gruffly.

"You ain't that damned dumb, even if you are a red devil," Barlow countered, grinning a little.

Once again Bull Heart was startled by the exchange, but this time he caught something in the eyes of each man that led him to believe that the words were meant to mask their true feelings for each other.

"Best red devil you ever met, mate," White Bear snapped, but he, too, grinned.

"Git goin', hoss, before those goddamn Blackfeet decide to wander on up here and inquire as to what we're yappin' about."

White Bear nodded and rose. He surveyed the glade

out there one more time through the looking glass before
giving the instrument back to Barlow. "Don't do nothin'
too bloody foolish, mate," he said. Then he turned and
stomped up the hill toward where the women had the
animals.

Lambert spun and hurried after him.

"You good man," Black Buffalo said. He grinned just
a bit. "For a white-eye devil."

Barlow looked at him, startled, then laughed a little.
"Jist keep that to mind, hoss, next time I need a bit of
help."

Black Buffalo nodded, then knelt next to Barlow.
With his knife blade, he swiftly sketched his planned
route in the dirt. He jabbed the knife into the dirt. "We
wait here for you," he said firmly. "Tomorrow night, we
be there. We wait till you come."

Barlow looked into the warrior's dark eyes and saw
humanity and true friendship there. He nodded. "Unless
them Blackfeet git me surrounded and make wolf bait
out of me, I'll be there, hoss."

"Good." Black Buffalo pulled his knife from the dirt
and slid it into the sheath. He rose and headed up the
hill, motioning for Bull Heart to follow him.

Instead, the young warrior squatted next to Barlow for
a moment and stared into his eyes. He liked this big
block of a white man. He clasped Barlow's shoulder
with a hand. "I avenge you if the Blackfeet take your
spirit," he said simply. Then, he, too, was up and gone,
heading for the animals.

Moments later, Raven Moon came by. She had tied
Beelzebub to the tree and then handed Barlow some
meat and jerky. She kissed him long and hard, and then
left, hurrying to catch up with the others.

"Well, Buffler, looks like we finally got us some
peace and quiet," Barlow said, petting the big dog, who
stretched out next to his master, enjoying the attention.

14

BUFFALO'S SOFT WHINE let Barlow know that the dog had picked up the scent of the Flathead camp. Barlow didn't know how far ahead it was, and in the darkness, he could see nothing, not even firelight. Either White Bear and the others were well hidden or yet some little distance away. He proceeded cautiously, slowly, listening intently, peering into the night for any sign of the camp.

Finally, he thought he spotted the flicker of a flame, and he pulled to a stop. He dismounted and knelt next to Buffalo. "Go on over there, boy," he said quietly, petting the big dog's head. "Go let White Bear know I'm here." He stood.

The dog hesitated only a moment, then trotted off, his tail waving in the dull moonlight.

Ten minutes later, White Bear—with Buffalo at his side—appeared out of the darkness. The two men shook hands. "Good to see you, old chap," the Shoshoni said with a grin.

"It plumb shines with this chil' to see your ugly face, too, hoss." He returned the grin.

"Come. Everyone's asleep—or was—but there's meat and coffee," White Bear said.

The two men and the dog walked slowly into the camp. Raven Moon and Far Thunder had heard something and were awake. Raven Moon kissed Barlow hard, letting him know how much she had missed him and worried about him. Then she took Beelzebub off the unsaddle the mule and brush it down.

Barlow and White Bear sat at one of the three small fires burning about the small camp. Far Thunder served them coffee and bark platters of deer meat. Barlow ate hungrily. He had not had real food except the little raw meat the others had left him and some jerky. By the time he had satisfied his hunger, Black Buffalo and Bull Heart had woken and joined him and White Bear.

"You have any trouble?" Black Buffalo asked.

"Nope," Barlow said, tossing away a bone. He thought back on it. He had waited at his spot for just a few minutes after the others had left, then moved up the hill a little ways. He sat behind a boulder, laying his rifle across the rock and settled in to wait. The position gave him an even better view of the field. The grass out where the Blackfeet were was belly-deep to a horse, and they could hide out there forever, should they choose. But as the grassland swept up toward the hill, the grass got shorter and shorter. None of the Blackfeet would be able to get within fifty yards of him without having to show himself.

Barlow gnawed on some raw meat as he watched and waited. Buffalo 2 sprawled next to him, sleeping, though his ears and nose twitched, sorting out the world around him.

Shortly before dark, Barlow spotted a few warriors grouped at the edge of the deep grass. Suddenly they bolted forward. Barlow threw his rifle up to his shoulder and fired, dropping one of the three Blackfeet. He swiftly reloaded, using the protection of the boulder against the arrows the Blackfeet were shooting at him.

Finished, Barlow leaned forward and snapped off another shot. He hit a second Blackfoot but was not all sure he had taken the warrior out permanently. Not that it mattered now—the third Blackfoot was almost on him, charging up the hill.

The Blackfoot was out of arrows and had tossed his bow aside, snatching out a toothed war club. He was so close now that Barlow could see the scowling face painted half in black, half in red.

Barlow jumped up, the action a bit awkward after his long bout of sitting, and he staggered backward, a little unbalanced. He tried to bring his rifle up to use it as a club against the Indian, but it was not necessary.

Buffalo bounded on the boulder and then leaped off, all of his great bulk and weight slamming into the Blackfoot's chest. As the warrior fell on his back and slid a few feet down the gentle slope of the hill, the Newfoundland tried to regain his footing, his paws raking deep, bloody furrows in the Indian's legs and torso.

The dog finally managed to stop, and then jumped forward, tearing a chunk out of the Blackfoot's arm as the warrior tried to get to his feet. Buffalo backed off a little, snarling, his muzzle coated with blood.

The warrior managed to stand and then spun and ran, hobbling down the hill as fast as he could.

Barlow called Buffalo back before the dog could chase after the Blackfoot. Instead, Barlow shot the Blackfoot with a pistol. With a sigh, Barlow reloaded his pistol and the rifle. Minutes later, with a last look down the ridge in the fast deepening dusk, he mounted Beelzebub. He moved out, heading in a direction that would take him increasingly farther from the trail used by White Bear and the others. He hoped that if the Blackfeet decided to follow that they would cut his tracks first and come after him rather than go after the others. He was certain he could outrun the Blackfeet if given a small head start.

He rode for several hours before he pulled to a stop in a small copse of trees and brush. He wearily unsaddled Beelzebub and brushed the mule down some, then hobbled him and let him graze. Exhausted, Barlow stretched out and fell asleep almost immediately, trusting in Buffalo's senses to alert him if any danger arose.

Shortly after dawn, he rode on, hungry and tired, but determined. After a couple of hours, he swung toward the northwest, heading for the trail the others had taken. He soon came to the stream that ran by the hill where he had stood off the Blackfeet. He clucked the mule down into the water and let the animal drink. Then they walked up the center of the shallow stream. For his part, Buffalo seemed to enjoy splashing around in the water. After more than a mile, Barlow pulled the mule out on the other bank and pushed on.

He saw no sign of the Blackfeet during the day, though he did cut the trail of White Bear and the Flatheads. By late afternoon, he picked up the pace, wanting to make his friends' camp before dark, if he could. But he was not as close as he had hoped, and it was not until after night had fallen that Buffalo alerted him to the presence of the camp.

"Do you think the Blackfoot've left off the chase?" White Bear asked, breaking Barlow from his reverie.

"I wouldn't wager on that, hoss. Hell, you know what obstinate devils them critters are. They ain't likely to

give up sich a chase for no reason. What I can't figure
is why they're so hellbent on trackin' us down."

"They have many reasons to want to raise hair on us,"
Black Buffalo said solemnly. "The People's friendship
with the Small Robes, the fact that we have defeated
them in battle many times, your search, Barlow. Many
things have blackened their hearts against us all."

"Reckon you're right," Barlow said with a shrug. "All
I know is that I'm plumb goddamn tired of these fractious bastards and their goddamn fractious ways."

"We all are, old chap," White Bear said. He paused.
"So, you think they're still on the trail after us?"

Barlow nodded. "Like Black Buffalo said—them bastards ain't gonna leave off this chase jist yet."

"Do we stand and fight?" Bull Heart asked, almost
eagerly. "Or go back and find them?"

"Hell, boy, that'd be plumb goddamn foolish," Barlow snapped. "Best we can do, I reckon, is to make it
to your village before they run us down again."

"How long till we get to your village, Black Buffalo?"
White Bear asked.

"Four suns," the Flathead leader responded. "If we
move fast."

"Then we'll move fast," Barlow said firmly. He
wanted to get this over with, get the Flatheads back to
their people so he could resume his search for Anna.
"And that means we all best git some robe time. We'll
be pullin' out afore first light."

They all headed toward their robes. As tired as Barlow
was, he was delighted to find that Raven Moon was
waiting for him, hungry for his touch. He smiled as he
stripped and then lay down next to her. "We ain't got
too much time for these doin's, you know, woman," he
said quietly as he stroked her cheek with a stubby finger.
"This ol' chil' needs some rest."

"You'll rest," Raven Moon promised. "When we're done, you'll rest good."

"You sound mighty sure of yourself, woman."

"Yes." She pulled his head down so she could kiss him passionately.

Fire arced from her tongue to his and sizzled through his body, strengthening and lengthening him almost instantly. He moaned around her mouth as his hands began roaming across her firm, eager flesh. He found her sweet spot and gently plied his fingers to it, while his mouth devoured hers.

Raven Moon's back soon arched with the sensations that flooded through her, and she ground her wet womanhood hard against his insistent hand, giving herself freely over to pleasurable feelings.

Barlow could wait no longer. He had to have her. He pushed her onto her back and swiftly moved up between her legs. He did not want to be rough, but he had little patience right now, and he was glad to see that she was open and waiting for him, as hungry for his manhood as he was for her femininity.

With her avid help, he was soon buried in her velvet cave and pumping hard in a rhythm of his own making. Raven Moon matched him beat for beat.

Within moments, Barlow was snuffling like a wounded grizzly as his climax slammed through his body and overflowed directly into hers. Raven Moon screeched softly, shuddering with the power of her own peak, which was expanded by her enjoyment of his elation.

"Goddamn," Barlow said soon after, still breathing heavily, as he lay on his back with Raven Moon ensconced in the cradle of his big shoulder, "if you don't sap a man in such a pleasurable way."

"Is good?" she asked, grinning against his chest.

"Very good!" Barlow exclaimed. He pulled the otter sleeping robe a little tighter around them both against the slight chill that was a harbinger of the rapidly approaching fall. And he fell asleep.

The group pulled out the next morning with the knowledge that another storm was heading their way. They could not, however, afford to take the time to sit it out. They all simply hoped that the storm would not be too bad and that it would pass quickly.

They rode as they had before—with Black Buffalo and White Bear in the lead, the women, children, Father Lambert and the extra animals, and then Barlow and Bull Heart bringing up the rear. They moved at a steady pace, fairly slow in deference to the animals and the children, but they made few stops during the day.

Two days later, Barlow was beginning to think they would make it to Black Buffalo's village without further trouble, when Buffalo began acting strangely, and Barlow knew something was up. He cursed silently.

Always observant and quick to learn, Bull Heart realized things were not as they should be. "Does Buffalo sense Blackfeet?" he asked.

Barlow shrugged. "Ain't sure, boy. But there's somethin' out there, sure as hell," he sighed. "And, I reckon this ol' chil' needs to go find out jist what it is. You make sure you keep your eyes peeled for trouble, boy," he warned. "If there are any goddamn Blackfeet around, they might be a sight closer than we think."

"I'll watch," Bull Heart said firmly. Silently, he hoped that the Blackfeet would show up. He wanted another chance to prove his mettle against such warriors. He had acquitted himself well in the battles against them before he and the others had been joined by Barlow and White Bear, but he wanted more honors, more glory. He had long dreamed of being the most recognized, most honored, most revered warrior of his people, not just his band. But seeing his friend Painted Elk go under at the hands of the Blackfeet had tempered his desires just a little. He was certain that he would fare better than Painted Elk, even though his friend had been a well-seasoned warrior.

Barlow moved slowly off, the big Newfoundland plodding beside him. The dog's nose was in the air, sniffing furiously. Barlow rode with one eye on the surrounding landscape and the other on the dog, watching for any signs or signals that Blackfeet were about.

It didn't take long before Buffalo seemed to really pick up some scent. Barlow stopped Beelzebub and watched the dog for a moment, trying to determine where the Indians—if there indeed were Indians out there—were. They were in another tall grass glade that ran about a hundred yards to a line of trees to the northeast. Behind him, moving through another glade just the other side of a thin stand of firs, were his friends. Barlow began to worry. If there were Blackfeet out there, and they were this close, he and the others could be in deep trouble.

Barlow dismounted and pulled out his collapsible telescope. He opened it and began surveying the landscape of the meadow. The light wind riffled the deep grass, and he saw nothing to indicate that anything was creating any kind of strange movement in the grass. He focused on the trees at the far side of the glade, studying them intently. He could spot nothing wrong.

"Goddammit, Buffler," he growled as he snapped the telescope closed, "where the hell are they? I know those bastards're out there somewhere."

The dog had sat, hidden in the deep grass, though he still seemed to be testing the air frequently and did not seem all that ready to relax. There was something out there, that much Barlow knew.

"C'mon, Buffler," he finally said. Taking Beelzebub's reins in hand, he walked swiftly toward where the others were traveling. When he reached the trees there, he mounted the mule, and took one last glance through the looking glass before riding on toward the head of the small column.

White Bear saw him and shouted to Black Buffalo. The two came toward him while the women kept the animals going on the trail.

"See something, old chap?" White Bear asked.

Barlow shook his head. "Buffler's actions and my own instincts tell me them boys are out there somewhere, and not very goddamn far, but I'll be damned if I can pick 'em out."

White Bear looked around, then shrugged. "Maybe we better get ready to make a stand, mate," he said.

"Might be best," Barlow agreed. He looked at Black Buffalo. "Any decent places nearby for sich doin's?" he asked.

"Nothing good," Black Buffalo allowed. "But we find something."

"We better," Barlow said dryly. "And goddamn soon."

15

A HAVEN OF sorts was in sight for the group when
the band of Blackfeet charged out of a stand of trees a
hundred yards away. The members of the group scrambled to get to safety.

At the rear, Barlow pulled Beelzebub to a halt and
slipped out of the saddle. "Go, Buffler!" he shouted.
"Git!"

The dog took off running, following the others.

Throwing his rifle over the saddle, Barlow aimed and
fired, reloaded, and fired again. He wasn't sure he had
hit anyone, but he did give the Blackfeet a moment's
pause, which would, Barlow hoped, be enough for his
friends—especially the women, children—to find sanctuary.

Not bothering to reload his rifle after the second shot,
Barlow swung up into the saddle and kicked the mule
into a run. Ahead of him, the others had reached cover.
The haven that had been forced on them was not the
place any of them would have picked had they been
given a choice. It consisted of an isolated stand of trees,

brush, and deadfalls with a front perhaps only twenty yards wide. The sole good point was that leading up to the copse was a short-grass meadow strewn with boulders, meaning the Blackfeet would have even less cover than Barlow's group.

Barlow thundered into the trees and slid off the mule before it had fully stopped. Raven Moon was there to grab the reins and take the beast back to where she and the other women were watching the animals. He hurried to find a spot behind a deadfall and set his unloaded rifle down.

The Blackfeet were almost on them. At least a dozen painted warriors charged ahead up the slight slope. Barlow yanked out the five-shot Colt Paterson and emptied it in a hurry at the invading Blackfeet. Two tumbled off their ponies, but both got up again moments later. Barlow never did see them get remounted—he and the others were too busy fending off the Blackfeet who were swarming through their little refuge, some still mounted, others who had slipped off their ponies and were charging on foot.

Barlow snatched out his two single-shot belt pistols and fired one after the other, hastily, without bothering to aim. The lead ball from one smashed into the stomach of one warrior, who was slammed backward by the blow. The other shot missed, and Barlow rolled several times out of the way, just as a Blackfoot jumped over the log and tried to impale him with his lance.

Barlow leaped up and swung one unloaded pistol at the Indian, who was stopped and turned and was yanking the lance free of the ground. The pistol barrel caught the warrior in the teeth, knocking several out, and staggering him. Without waiting for the Blackfoot to regain his equilibrium, Barlow moved in on the warrior and battered him senseless with the pistol.

With a ferocious snarl, Buffalo charged and jumped onto another Blackfoot who was just about to bludgeon Barlow in the back of the head with a war club. The warrior went down with a shriek of surprise, as the New-foundland tore at his flailing arms and legs.

Barlow spun and noted the dog's attack on the enemy in one swift glance, and then surged toward another Blackfoot who was heading for the animals. Barlow pulled his tomahawk as he ran and chopped the Black-foot down before the warrior even knew he was there.

Barlow rose and turned, taking in the battlefield. It was obvious that White Bear, Black Buffalo, and Bull Heart had acquitted themselves well. Several Blackfoot bodies lay strewn about. The surviving Blackfeet were fleeing, having scooped up some of their dead and wounded, but leaving others that were too difficult to get to right now.

Barlow breathed heavily as he watched the Blackfeet race off toward another stand of trees across the meadow. He wiped the blade of the tomahawk on the shirt of the Blackfoot at his feet and slid away. Then he slowly walked over to the log behind which he had hidden and picked up his weapons. One by one, he reloaded the two belt pistols, the Colt Paterson, and the powerful Henry ri-fle. As he was doing so, the three other men walked up.

Bull Heart yipped a war cry. "How do you say it?" he said. "We showed 'em, didn't we?" He was almost ecstatic.

"That we did, boy," Barlow said tiredly. "That we did. But don't you go gittin' too rhapsodic over it, hoss. Them critters'll be back, I reckon."

"You think so?" Bull Heart asked, unconcerned.

"It's a certainty, old chap," White Bear said evenly.

"How are you sure?" the young warrior asked.

"We're damned close to your village, old chap," White Bear said. "The Blackfeet don't have much time left to take us. And they wouldn't have chased us all this way if they weren't determined to raise our hair. Aye, mate, they'll be back."

"Then let 'em come," Bull Heart said cockily. "We've turned 'em away once, we can do it again."

Barlow shook his head. He understood how the young man felt; he had felt the same himself when he was younger. He just wished the youth could see what he could see now—that battle was not the glorious activity he thought it was. But Barlow knew that would not happen. Not anytime soon. Bull Heart would learn it for himself—if he lived long enough.

Barlow leaned his rifle against the log, on which he now sat. "I reckon those critters'll leave us be for a spell, though," he said. "We bloodied 'em pretty good, and I expect they're gonna wait till dark, at least. Maybe even till mornin'."

"We sit and wait then, old chap?" White Bear asked.

Barlow nodded. "Ain't no use in runnin'," he said. "They can catch up to us pretty quick, should they desire. And, while this ain't the best place for makin' a stand, it's at least somethin'. And we don't know what we'll find out on the trail, if anything." He stood. "You keep a watch out for them devils," he said to Black Buffalo and Bull Heart. "Me and White Bear are gonna go check on the animals."

The two—accompanied by Buffalo—headed deeper into the trees. The women reported that everything was all right, that no one was injured, and that they had lost no animals. Raven Moon told Barlow that no Blackfeet had even gotten close to them.

Barlow nodded, satisfied. "Some of you women best git a fire goin' and set some meat to cookin'. It looks like we might be here a spell, and we know them Black-feet're gonna come again. We'll need our strength. The rest of you can keep the animals in check whilst we watch out for those Blackfeet."

The women hurried to their various tasks, while Barlow, White Bear, and the dog went back to the edge of the trees. Black Buffalo and Bull Heart had already moved apart and were sitting—the former resting against a log, the latter leaning against a boulder—watching the gentle downward slope. The meadow spread as far as they could see to the left and right, so the Blackfeet would have a hard time trying to go around and sneak up from their west.

White Bear moved off to the left, beyond Black Buffalo; Barlow went to the right, to where he had been before. He settled down in front of the log deadfall this time, resting against it. Buffalo lay next to him, his head in Barlow's lap. Barlow petted the big dog.

Barlow was glad when Raven Moon brought him some cooked elk meat and a mug of coffee. He had been perilously close to falling asleep in the heat and monotony of the afternoon. Raven Moon left but returned a few minutes later with another bark platter of meat for herself. She sat next to Barlow, and they ate quietly, feeding pieces of gristle and meat to the dog, who gobbled them down greedily.

After Barlow had eaten his fill, Raven Moon went back to join the other women. Barlow walked with her and retrieved his telescope from the sack on his horse, then returned to his spot at the log. He used the looking glass to scan the stand of trees across the meadow. He could see shadowy movements among the trees, so he knew the Blackfeet were still there, but he could not tell really what they were doing or how many of them there were.

The afternoon dragged on, the heat and monotony unbroken by the breeze or the gnats or anything else. Barlow checked the other stand of trees periodically through the telescope, but nothing out of the ordinary happened.

As dusk began to fall, Barlow rose and walked toward Bull Heart, stopping and kneeling next to the Flathead. "You take the first watch fer the night, boy," he said. "You wake Black Buffalo after about three hours. You understand?"

Bull Heart nodded.

"And don't do nothin' foolish, hoss." Barlow rose and went to Black Buffalo. "Bull Heart's gonna take first watch and then git you in three hours or so. You git White Bear about three hours after and git back to sleep yourself."

Black Buffalo nodded, stood, and headed farther back into the trees to sleep.

Finally, Barlow went to White Bear and told him to take the watch when Black Buffalo woke him, and that he was to get Barlow up after about a three-hour stretch.

"Right, old chap," White Bear said. He rose and stretched. "You expectin' them to attack just after dawn?"

"Yep. I figure they'll start creepin' up this way jist afore dawn till they're real close. Then, with first light, they'll attack, thinkin' to catch us by surprise."

"My thinking, too, mate. But I think it's going to be them who gets the surprise."

"That's what I plan for 'em."

The two headed into the trees and spread out their sleeping robes. The women were bedding down, the horses and mules were hobbled enough to keep them from straying, and Bull Heart was on the lookout. Barlow fell asleep almost instantly. He woke, however, at the slight sounds of Bull Heart waking Black Buffalo a few hours later. He waited there until Black Buffalo had moved off with a mug of coffee to take his spot on lookout. Then Barlow rose and padded silently around the camp, checking the animals, making sure the women were fine.

He was still restless, but he forced himself to lay down again. Still, he couldn't sleep now, at least not right away. He was eager to get this battle over with and get the Flatheads back to their village so he could get on Anna's trail again. She seemed, at times like this, to be getting dimmer and dimmer in his memory, and that irritated and frightened him. He could not—would not—allow her memory to fade.

Barlow finally fell asleep again, but it seemed like only minutes before Black Buffalo came along and roused White Bear for the watch, which also woke him again. Once more he toured the camp, but then he decided he'd just as well stay up. He went to the fire and poured himself some coffee. Taking some meat, he moved out of the firelight and ate and drank, passing the time until it was his turn to take over as sentry. Buffalo had wandered around with him, but finally decided he'd lay down and sleep again near where Barlow was sitting.

Finally, White Bear came looking for Barlow. Hearing the Shoshoni, Barlow moved back toward his sleeping robe, and as White Bear neared, he said, "I'm up, hoss."

"Good. Need coffee, old chap?"

"Had some, but I reckon a bit more won't hurt none."

The two walked to the fire and filled their mugs. As they sipped, White Bear said, "I think I'll just stay awake and keep you company, old chap. If you don't mind."

"Reckon that suits this ol' chil'." He would be happy to have someone like White Bear out there with him, knowing that the Blackfeet were going to attack soon.

"You see any sign of the priest?" White Bear asked.

Barlow almost laughed. "That chil's slept through all this. I never expected any different from him, though."

They finished their coffee and wove through the dark trees toward the edge of the meadow. They stayed within a few feet of each other, though, instead of spreading out. And they waited, their senses heightened, staring into the deep darkness as the stars faded from view.

As the first faint grayness edged into the sky to the east, White Bear sidled up alongside Barlow. "I'm going to go wake Black Buffalo and Bull Heart," he said.

"Good. It'll be better if they was—"

"No need, friends," Black Buffalo said from just behind them. "We're here." He had made sure he woke to be back on guard about this time and had gotten young Bull Heart.

"That shines." Barlow said. "Best spread out, and be ready. I expect those damned devils'll be comin' at us right quick here." The others moved off, and Barlow shifted his position so he was behind the log again. The grayness continued to edge out the black until the landscape took on a surreal look. It was then that the Blackfeet attacked.

The warriors came in a silent rush, suddenly appearing out of the gloom, their painted faces and the gray morning making a frightening spectacle.

Barlow fired the Colt deliberately, aiming at the shadowy figures that suddenly loomed up in front of him as if out of nowhere. Of five shots, three hit enemy warriors, two of whom stayed down. Other warriors swarmed over him as he rose up from behind the log. He slammed one down with a forearm to the head; Buffalo 2 plowed into another, sending him sprawling.

Barlow kicked the third one in the stomach, but it

barely brushed the warrior, who lashed out with a war club. It whistled past Barlow's shoulder and head as he ducked. The Blackfoot leaped forward and used the shield strapped to his left forearm to push Barlow backward. Barlow's heel hit a stone, and he tumbled backward, falling hard and heavily, his head glancing off the log that had given him shelter.

Before Barlow could get up, the Blackfoot had jumped on him. Only Buffalo's quick rush and his powerful bite on the warrior's arm kept the enemy's war club from shattering Barlow's head.

The huge dog growled and tugged the warrior off Barlow, at least enough for Barlow to rise. Without delay, while the Blackfoot was still struggling to get free of the determined dog, Barlow split his skull with his tomahawk.

The Indian fell dead, and Buffalo let go of his arm.

Barlow spun to see two more Blackfeet charging at him from just a few feet away. He headed for one, while Buffalo raced to attack the other. It was over in moments as the Newfoundland went straight for the throat, and his master simply hacked his foe to a quick death with his tomahawk.

As Buffalo continued to maul the warrior, Barlow took a fast look around. The sky was now more pink than gray, and he could see that his three friends had done well again. The Blackfeet were fleeing once more. As Barlow began to relax a little, a solitary Blackfoot burst out of the deeper trees, driving several ponies and mules ahead of him. And across his own pony was Yellow Leaf.

16

RAVEN MOON WAS only moments behind, screaming at the loss of her daughter. Barlow ignored her as he shoved his bloody tomahawk away and snatched up his rifle. Then he spun and knelt, bringing the rifle up to his shoulder. Drawing a bead, he squeezed the trigger. The big rifle boomed, and as the powder smoke cleared, Barlow could see that the Blackfoot was hit but still clinging onto his pony.

Barlow threw down his rifle, turned, and ran hellbent for the animals. There he jumped on Beelzebub bareback. "C'mon, you goddamn stubborn ol' mule," he roared as he grabbed a fistful of mane. He kicked his heels into the mule's side, and the animal bolted.

They roared out of the trees, down the slight slope, and across the grassland. The Blackfoot had fallen off his pony, but the animal was still running, though not as fast, because the stolen animals had slowed with no one driving them. Little Yellow Leaf was holding on to the pony's mane and neck for dear life.

Barlow urged a little more speed out of the mule and

began rapidly closing the gap with the runaway pony, which was decelerating even more as the small stolen herd eased its speed considerably, until the Blackfoot horse was virtually a part of the pack. With a final burst of speed, Barlow pulled alongside the pony and with one hand plucked Yellow Leaf off it and pulled her onto Beelzebub. She sat in front of Barlow. He shouted and yelled at the stolen animals and managed to get them to start to turn in a wide circle.

As Barlow got the animals going back toward his camp, he noticed White Bear, Black Buffalo, and Bull Heart racing toward him on their own ponies. Barlow glanced over his shoulder and saw that several Blackfeet had come out of the trees on that side and were charging at him. A few arrows fell around him, not hitting him.

His three friends began firing arrows themselves, and within moments the Blackfeet had turned back. Soon after, the two Flatheads and the Shoshoni had almost circled Barlow and the stolen mules and horses. With such an escort, the short ride back to their refuge was made hurriedly.

Once back in the trees, Barlow handed Yellow Leaf down to her mother, who nearly smothered her with loving, relieved embraces. She carried the child away to share some moments alone with her.

With White Bear and Barlow standing watch, Black Buffalo and Bull Heart took the animals back to the rest of their herd. Then the two Flatheads joined their two friends.

"What now?" Bull Heart asked.

"I ain't sure, hoss," Barlow said. He was staring across the meadow, wondering. He did not think the Blackfeet would try another attack now that it was full light. But he did not think they would give up, either. The thought of sitting here another day was displeasing, but the thought of leaving and getting caught by the Blackfeet out in the open was even more disturbing.

In the silence, White Bear picked up Barlow's telescope and began viewing the Blackfeet camp across the meadow. Suddenly, he started, staring hard through the glass. "They're leaving, mates," he said in surprise.

"The hell you say, hoss," Barlow snapped, jumping up. He grabbed the telescope from White Bear and peered through it. "Well, I'll be goddamned," he muttered, astonished. "I never thought they'd jist give up and leave." He looked through the glass a bit longer before handing it to Black Buffalo, who assured himself that it was true.

"Now we leave," Black Buffalo said as he handed the 'scope back to Barlow.

"Reckon not, hoss," Barlow said, sitting again. He collapsed the looking glass and tapped it against a palm. "Not jist yet anyway."

"Why?" Bull Heart asked. "They're gone, and we're close to our People. A day's march and we'll be there."

"Because I don't trust them critters, hoss," Barlow said flatly. "Not one goddamn little bit." He paused, then ordered, "Now, go git some rest, all of you. I'll keep watch."

"You sure, old chap?"

"Yep, I'll wake you all in a few hours at most. Then we can decide what to do."

True to his word, Barlow woke the others three hours later. When he had gathered them at the fire and they were drinking coffee and eating more elk meat, Barlow said, "I've still seen no sign of those devils, but I still don't trust 'em. Bull Heart, I want you to head on over there and see if they've really left or just maybe pulled back a ways."

The young Flathead warrior nodded, proud to have

been given such an important task. He rose, ready to leave.

"Don't take no goddamn chances, boy," Barlow said. "And don't do nothin' foolish. And, if they're really gone, don't follow too long. I expect you back here soon after the sun reaches its height. Understand?"

Bull Heart nodded again, eager to be on his way. When he realized that there would be no more instructions, he turned and got his pony. With his bow in hand, quiver of arrows across his back, he swung onto the horse and rode out.

"You think they're really gone, old chap?" White Bear asked.

Barlow shrugged. "I'd have bet my life that they wouldn't leave," he said carefully. "But who knows with those damn critters. Maybe they figured their medicine has gone bad on 'em. Maybe it's jist a trick."

"The Blackfeet are determined warriors," Black Buffalo said. "They don't give up easily."

Barlow nodded. "I know. That's what makes me think they might be up to some goddamn trickery." He sighed. "Well, we can only wait now, till Bull Heart returns."

"You better get some sleep, old chap," White Bear said. "You look coopered."

Barlow nodded again. "A plumb shinin' idee, hoss," he said. He rose and headed for his sleeping robe, where Raven Moon awaited him. Their lovemaking was perfunctory, however, because he was exhausted, and she was still recovering from having come so close to losing her daughter. They were satisfied, though, in each other's warm comfort.

Barlow awoke foggily when White Bear shook him. "Bull Heart's back," the Shoshoni said.

Barlow sat up and rubbed his face. The nap had not been as refreshing as he had hoped it would be. He nodded gratefully when White Bear stuck a mug of hot, black coffee in his hand. He sipped a bit, realizing that Raven Moon was not there. She must have gotten up already and was with the other women. He set the mug down, rose, and hastily dressed. He grabbed his coffee and with White Bear on one side and Buffalo on the other, headed for the fire. "Well?" he asked as he sat.

"The Blackfeet are gone," Bull Heart announced solemnly.

"You're sure?" Barlow demanded.

"Yes. I follow 'em two miles. Can't see 'em anywhere."

Barlow nodded. "It surprises the hell out of me," he said. "But so be it. If those critters're gone, we might's well pack up and move on. Soon. With any luck, we can make the village by this time tomorrow or so."

"We'll have to push it, old chap."

"Then we'll push it," Barlow snapped. He was still tired and of no mind to be reasonable. He was tired of this whole ordeal, but mostly he was tired of not being able to find Anna. Even worse, he was unable to even have the chance to find his daughter. Something always got in the way. He wanted to be shed of the Flatheads. Not that he didn't care for them. He just wanted to get them back home so he could return to his real quest.

"Then let's go, mates," White Bear said. "There's work to be done. You set there, old chap, and finish your coffee. Maybe have some meat. We'll get things ready."

Barlow nodded in appreciation as the others hurried off. Soon the camp was a bustle, with supplies being loaded, animals saddled, pack animals roped together. Barlow was barely finished with his meal when everyone was ready to go. He rose, checked his weapons and gear, then mounted Beelzebub. "Black Buffalo, you and

White Bear can have the honors of leadin' the way again," he said.

The Flathead and the Shoshoni pulled out. Moments afterward, the women—and the priest—pushing the animals ahead of them, rode out, followed a minute later by Barlow and Bull Heart. The stand of trees they rode through was only a few hundred yards deep, and then they were in another mountain meadow. The grass was brown now, so late in the summer, and fairly short. Peaks arose in the distance in all directions. Small clumps of trees could be seen now and again. Herds of elk fled at their advance, as did solitary grizzly bears and large moose, their antlers just starting to really grow. They pushed fairly hard across the open expanse, trying to make up time. Black Buffalo had said he knew of a place to spend the night that would provide a good camp, but it was normally almost a full day's travel, and they had not even pulled out until shortly after noon.

Several hours after they had left their small haven, Barlow began to get that itch in his shoulder blades again, that sign that something was not right. It had never failed him, and he paid heed to it now. "I'll be back directly," he said tersely to Bull Heart, and he trotted off, Buffalo accompanying him.

Instinct and experience turned him toward a stand of trees lining a stream to the northeast. As he neared it, he slowed Beelzebub and finally stopped. He searched the area with his looking glass but saw nothing. He rode on until he reached the trees and began weaving his way through them, following the stream eastward. After riding half a mile without seeing anyone, he turned back and rode out southwest, across the meadow toward his small traveling party.

As he returned to his place at the rear of the column alongside Bull Heart, Barlow still felt uncomfortable, and it was annoying him. He split off again, and rode southward a little ways, but there were no trees or anything within any short distance that could hide a group of Blackfeet. He returned once again to the travelers. But he worried as the nagging feeling continued to sit on his shoulders like a cape.

They angled slightly toward the northwest, away from a thick hump of rock that seemed shot straight up out of the ground, a tall, jagged peak that had a forbidding aura. As the meadow narrowed between the treelined stream and the jagged tor, Barlow's agitation increased. Something was not right, but he could not figure out what it was.

Then a number of Blackfeet burst out of the trees along the stream, racing across the short distance to the travelers, who had no place to hide now.

"Son of a bitch!" Barlow cursed, mostly at himself. He had not thought to check westward along the line of trees, not thinking that the Blackfeet would have had enough time to circle around and then pass them up, considering where they had started.

The group stopped and, without orders, fell into a defensive posture. The women gathered up the animals and kept themselves and the children in the midst of them, using the horse and mule flesh for protection. Father Lambert helped them as much as he could bring himself to do.

The four fighting men fanned out a little, dismounting. Barlow knelt and fired his rifle, taking down one of the Blackfeet at a hundred yards. He managed to get off another shot, wounding an enemy warrior before the Blackfeet were too close for him to make much use of the rifle. He pulled his belt pistols and quickly sprawled out on his stomach, making himself as small a target as possible. He fired the two pistols carefully, but the charging Blackfeet made poor targets, and he hit no one. He cursed himself again and then went to work with the Colt Paterson. Though it was a smaller weapon, the Blackfeet were closer, and he had somewhat better results with the five-shot revolver.

White Bear and the two Flatheads were firing arrows carefully, having a little more success than Barlow had had with his pistols. Between them, they had cut the number of Blackfeet down considerably.

Through it all, Buffalo raced back and forth near Barlow, growling and barking. He managed to stay out of the way of Blackfeet arrows, a number of which were directed at him.

The Blackfeet finally turned and raced for the safety of the trees. Barlow took this opportunity to reload his pistols. He stood and looked around but could see no place that would be defensible by his little group. He wondered how many more Blackfeet were left. Between the battle yesterday and this morning, and now this one, he and his warrior friends had killed or wounded quite a few enemies. He did not think they could keep up such losses much longer. On the other hand, another charge or two by the Blackfeet might be enough to overwhelm Barlow and his friends. White Bear, Black Buffalo, and Bull Heart, not having had a chance to recover the arrows they had already used, were running short of them.

Barlow was fortunate that Beelzebub had not moved far from where Barlow had dismounted from the mule. The big beast stood munching the short, brown grass just a few feet away. Barlow went to it and pulled out his telescope. He extended it to full length and began perusing the tree line. Suddenly he started. "Damn," he muttered. He looked through the glass again, then shouted, "White Bear, c'mon over here!"

When the Shoshoni trotted up, Barlow handed him

the telescope. "Take a look over yonder and tell me what you see."

A little surprised, White Bear peered through the long tube. "Blackfeet, old chap," he said after a moment. He could not understand Barlow's apparent consternation.

"Look again, boy," Barlow ordered. "See that pine yonder with the twisted up branch near the bottom?" When White Bear nodded, Barlow added, "Look there. And closely."

White Bear did as he was told. After a moment, he started to bring the glass down from his eye, ready to demand that Barlow tell him what it was he was looking for. Then he stopped and looked through the telescope again, peering intently.

"See somethin'?" Black Buffalo asked as he and an equally curious Bull Heart strode up, wondering what was going on.

White Bear brought the glass down and looked at Barlow. "I'll be damned," he muttered.

Barlow smiled grimly. "My thought exactly."

"What is it?" Black Buffalo demanded in irritation. He hated that anything was kept from him.

"Look for yourself, old chap," White Bear said, handing the telescope to the Flathead leader.

Black Buffalo's eyebrows rose, but he took the looking glass and peered through it. He mumbled something in his own language.

"What is it?" Bull Heart asked, not liking being the only one not knowing what had been seen.

"Four Dogs and Big Eagle are with the Blackfeet over there, hoss," Barlow said sharply.

"The Small Robes?"

Barlow nodded.

17

"WHAT THE HELL are those two bloody buggers doing with the Blackfeet?" White Bear wondered aloud.

"Tryin' to gain their goddamn favor I reckon," Barlow snapped. "It's the only thing that makes any sense."

"Must be," Black Buffalo interjected. He was furious at having been deceived by the two warriors. He turned to stare across the sward, eyes burning hotly. Only the wisdom of his years and experience kept him from donning his war paint and riding over there and challenging not only the Blackfeet, but the two Small Robes. He turned back toward his friends. "They must pay for this," he growled.

"Yep," Barlow allowed. "And they will, goddammit."

White Bear and Bull Heart nodded in avid agreement.

Barlow took another look through the glass, then collapsed it down into itself. "We best move on as best we can," he said. "We'll stay together, move slow, be alert. It looks like this meadow narrows down some more between that peak and the stream. At its narrowest is where we'll be in the most danger. I figure that's when they'll attack again."

The men mounted up. Black Buffalo told the women and Father Lambert what was planned, and then they moved out. They went slowly, keeping together. The four fighting men rode in single file on the north side of the group, between the travelers and the Blackfeet who were in the trees along the river.

Barlow stopped briefly every few yards and looked through his telescope. The Blackfeet were moving along with his group, staying within the trees, but pacing the Flathead group. It reinforced Barlow's thought that they would attack again soon.

Barlow tensed as the group neared the narrow neck of land between the peak and the stream. He glanced over the column. The women, children, priest, and animals were in a tight bunch, as safe as they could be under the circumstances. Bull Heart rode ahead of him, with White Bear next toward the front, with Black Buffalo ahead of him in the lead. They rode about five yards apart. Buffalo 2 trotted alongside Beelzebub, tongue lolling.

The attack came perhaps five minutes and fifty yards later than Barlow had expected, but it came in a fast, relatively silent rush—no war cries or shouts, just the pounding of unshod hooves and the hiss of arrows.

The group stopped and the fighting men swung off their mounts to face the onrushing Blackfeet horde. Barlow knelt and fired his rifle, but missed his target—the Blackfeet were already just about on top of them. He dropped the rifle and pulled out the revolver. Two shots took out the nearest warrior, but then Barlow had to dive out of the way as another mounted Blackfoot swooped down on him and tried to pin him to the ground with a lance. Barlow rolled several times and ended up on his

back, facing his group. He brought the pistol up and
fired at the warrior who had just tried to impale him.
Two shots slammed into the Indian's back, and he tumbled to the ground.

Blackfeet swarmed around the traveling group, firing
arrows whenever possible without endangering their
compatriots, trying to kill the fighting men with club or
lance, maneuvering to drive off the extra horses and
mules and hoping to capture the women and children.

A racing warrior slammed Barlow on the back as he
galloped past, the blow knocking Barlow down. Only
his massive shoulder muscles saved him, but he would
be sore for some time.

He scrambled up and snapped off the final shot from
his revolver, which punctured the attacking warrior's
arm but did not unseat him. The Blackfoot had whirled
his pony and was ready to attack Barlow again. The lead
ball in his arm seemed not to slow him down much, as
it was the arm that held his shield. He charged, racing
toward Barlow, who calmly stood his ground, pulled a
belt pistol, and fired the single shot.

The ball plowed into the Blackfoot's chest and the
Indian rolled head over heels off the back of his pony,
landing with a thud in the grass.

Barlow turned, and a moment later a Blackfoot
jumped off his pony onto Barlow. They tumbled to the
ground, wrestling and grappling, each trying to gain a
grip or an edge on the other. The Blackfoot had dropped
his war club as he pounced on Barlow, and now he
scrambled to pull his knife, which he finally managed to
do.

Barlow grabbed the warrior's knife arm by the wrist
and twisted it as hard as he could with his limited lev-
erage. His power, though, was enough to move the knife
away from his neck. Barlow flailed around until he

latched his other hand on the warrior's ear and he pulled with all the might he could muster.

The Indian's head moved slowly to the side. Then, using the strength in his torso and legs, Barlow managed to roll the Blackfoot off of him. He gave a last shove and then jumped up. As the warrior began to rise again, Barlow slammed him on the side of the face with an enormous fist, breaking his cheekbone and eye socket. The Indian slumped to the dirt, a soft grunt the only acknowledgement of his pain.

Barlow yanked out his tomahawk, knelt, and dispatched the warrior with a swift strike to the head. Then he rose and looked around. Black Buffalo and White Bear seemed to be holding their own, but Bull Heart was nearly being overwhelmed by three Blackfeet.

"Buffler!" Barlow bellowed. "Help Bull Heart! Go!"

The dog, who had been chewing on a downed Blackfoot, looked up, then darted toward the young Flathead.

Barlow ran that way, too, but he was well behind the dog, who tore a chunk out of the back of a Blackfoot's thigh.

The warrior bellowed in pain and rage as he swung around, war club in hand. He swung viciously at Buffalo's head, but the dog easily dashed out of the way, then rushed back in, grabbing the warrior's arm in his powerful jaws and clamping down. The Blackfoot fought back as best he could, but he was hampered by the shield he wore on his left arm, and the inability to free his right arm—the one with his weapon—from the dog's muscular grip.

The dog backed up, his mighty body hauling the Blackfoot with him, away from Bull Heart. He let go, then, and raced in on the warrior, fangs searching for the Blackfoot's throat. The dog's great weight knocked the warrior down, and the Newfoundland suddenly had free rein to tear the Indian apart.

Just after Buffalo had tugged the Blackfoot away from Bull Heart, Barlow arrived and leaped. His big, bulky body plowed into Bull Heart and the two Blackfeet, bowling them all over in one churning mass of torsos, arms and legs. All four men scrambled up and warily faced each other.

Barlow's opponent was a tall, broad-shouldered warrior. His face and bare chest were streaked with stripes of black and red paint. His dark eyes glittered as he waved his stone-headed war club in front of him.

Barlow still had his tomahawk in hand, and it continued to drop blood from the last Blackfoot who had moments ago died under the sharp blade.

Slightly bent, the two men moved back and forth cautiously, taking each other's measure. But Barlow knew he could not afford to waste time, and he charged, swinging the tomahawk in great looping arcs.

Using his shield for protection, the Blackfoot slowly gave way, backing up steadily. Barlow continued to pound away at him with the sharp weapon. Finally, the war shield fractured and then splintered in shreds. The blow that smashed the shield to the ground also shattered the warrior's forearm.

With his left arm hanging mostly useless at his side, the Blackfoot tried to bring the attack to Barlow, flailing wildly at the white man with his war club. But Barlow managed to block the blows by jamming his forearm up against the Indian's. Then he hacked the Blackfoot several times with his tomahawk, chopping his face and head into a bloody mask. The warrior fell, dead.

Barlow looked around. Bull Heart had slain the warrior he had faced and had rushed off to aid Black Buffalo, and the two were battling a pair of Blackfeet. White

Bear still appeared to be doing well, especially now that Buffalo had just raced there to help him. Some Blackfeet were heading back for the trees, picking up some of their dead and wounded as they rode.

A scream made him jerk around, looking toward the herd. He was sure it was Raven Moon who had screamed. Two Blackfeet were there. One was trying to get the animals loose from each other to be able to drive them off. The other had grabbed Blue Beads, Little Star Woman's seven-year-old daughter, and was attempting to haul the girl up on to his pony.

"White Bear!" he roared. He pointed when the Shoshoni looked at him. Both began racing toward where the women were struggling to keep control over the animals.

Blue Beads was fighting fiercely, trying to get out of the grip of the mounted Blackfoot warrior. She kicked and screeched, though she was having little success in freeing herself.

Her mother raced out from the midst of the animals and attacked the warrior, scratching and clawing at his bare legs, back, and stomach. The Blackfoot kicked the women in the chest, sending her reeling. Then he slid off the horse on the other side—where he held Blue Beads. He cuffed the girl with a backhand but still did not let her go. He pulled out his knife, ready to plunge it into the girl.

Barlow saw it but knew he was still much too far away to be of any use. His breath caught in his throat as he tried to put on an extra burst of speed, but even then he knew he would never be in time to save the young girl. A sick feeling sprang up in his stomach and spread through his body, squeezing his chest. He wished he still had his last belt pistol on him, even though at this distance there would be as much chance of hitting the girl as there was of striking the warrior. But the weapon had fallen out in one of his tussles with one of the Blackfeet.

Then Father Sylvestre Lambert suddenly burst out from the protection of the equines. With no regard for his own life, he slammed into the Blackfoot, grabbing hold of the man's knife arm. He strained to get the warrior to drop the blade, but the Blackfoot instead released Blue Beads and used that hand—balled into a fist—to pummel the priest's face and head.

Lambert fell under the flood of blows, sagging to the grass with a heavy groan.

The Blackfoot kicked the priest in the face and then spun toward Blue Beads again.

The girl, who had been pulling against the warrior's iron grip, had fallen when he released her, and her head hit the ground, stunning her a little. She was unable to move as the warrior reached down and grabbed a handful of her long black, unfettered hair. He raised the knife again.

Somehow, Father Lambert managed to get up and jumped at the Blackfoot, once more grabbing his knife arm and trying to wrestle the blade away from the warrior. Again he was well overmatched against the muscular, experienced warrior. The Blackfoot pounded him on the side of the face with a hard left fist, staggering the priest. Then the knife arm lashed out, and the blade slid shallowly across Lambert's chest, opening a thin red trench under his cassock.

The Blackfoot plunged his blade into Lambert's breast and pulled it free as the priest fell backward. The warrior turned back toward the girl, but her mother had raced around to her and managed to get her to her feet and away from the furious warrior.

Even more enraged, the Blackfoot spun back and

kicked Lambert, then stabbed him twice more in the chest and again in the stomach. He stood, looking around for another target, someone on whom to take out his anger.

Barlow, still running, watched it all with a feeling of dread and helplessness sweeping over him. He was marginally relieved when he saw Little Star Woman get Blue Beads to relative safety, but he was horrified at the Blackfoot's treatment of the priest. While he had little liking for the Jesuit, he did not like seeing anyone die like that, especially after that person had just risked his life to save a child.

Barlow plowed into the warrior who had killed Lambert, smashing him to the ground on his face. He managed to keep on his feet, though he stumbled forward a few steps. He stopped and turned in time to kick the Indian in the side as the Blackfoot tried to get up. The warrior was lifted and flipped, landing on his back.

"No good, red devil, son of a bitch!" Barlow said as he knelt next to the Indian. Using the tomahawk he still carried in his hand, he hacked away at the man's head and throat.

White Bear ran up and pulled the enraged Barlow away from the Blackfoot, yelling, "That's enough, old chap. He's bloody gone under, now let him be."

Barlow slowly regained his senses and stood there breathing heavily. "Goddamn, these doin's don't shine with this goddamn chil' no more," Barlow snapped. "These goddamn devilish Blackfeet've done the last of their damage to us, hoss."

White Bear nodded. "I think it is time we put a bloody end to their gammy actions, old chap."

Things had calmed down now. All the Blackfeet—including the one who had been trying to run off with the animals—had fled.

Black Buffalo and Bull Heart walked up, looking weary but unbowed. Moments later Buffalo trotted up to the group, his muzzle still covered with blood. Barlow patted the big dog on the head. "You done good, boy," he said quietly.

"What do we do with him, old chap?" White Bear asked, nodding toward Lambert's body.

Barlow thought for a moment, then asked, "You mind if he was buried near your village, Black Buffalo?"

The Flathead leader raised his eyebrows in surprise. He had never expected Barlow to take such a friendly attitude toward the priest.

"I might not've thought much of him before, hoss," Barlow explained. "But he went under savin' little Blue Beads. It weren't for him, she'd be the one layin' there now, 'stead of him. I reckon that riskin' his hair to save her has redeemed him considerably and, as such, he deserves a decent buryin'." He paused. "So, what do you say, hoss?"

Black Buffalo nodded without hesitation.

"Good," Barlow said. He sighed, weary of all the fighting, of all the troubles, yet knowing that it wasn't over. "Anybody hurt?" he asked.

Everyone shook his head. Barlow ignored the pain in his shoulders from the blow he had taken. He was losing no blood, and he didn't think any bones were broken, so he would live with it. The women and children were all right, too.

"What now?" Black Buffalo asked.

"First," Barlow responded, "we regroup as far as our weapons go. Then we'll pay the goddamn Blackfeet a visit."

18

"WHAT I AIM to do," Barlow said as the four men stood on the grass looking toward where the Blackfeet were still lurking in the trees along the stream, "is to send what Blackfeet I can to the Happy Huntin' Ground and send the rest of 'em packin'. Except for Big Eagle and Four Dogs. I want those two bastards alive."

The others nodded. They were grim of face, determined of heart. Barlow had retrieved and reloaded all his guns; the warriors had gone out and picked up all their arrows that they could find, as well as ones from the Blackfeet. Their own supply of arrows had been pretty deleted over the past day or two, and they were happy to take replacements wherever they could find them.

"One other thing, boys," Barlow said. "We need someone to stay behind—to watch over the women, children, and animals. And to get them all home, if somethin' should happen to us."

"You will stay behind, Bull Heart," Black Buffalo said sternly.

The young warrior considered arguing, but dropped the notion when he saw the look on Black Buffalo's face. The elder Flathead looked more fierce than Bull Heart had ever seen. While he did not like the idea of being left behind to tend to the women and children, he knew that debating it here and now would do nothing but anger Black Buffalo, as well as Barlow and White Bear. He nodded, trying to assuage his anger with the knowledge that the task he had been given could very well turn out to be important.

The three older men went to the women and said good-bye, then mounted their animals.

"Are we just going to ride on over there, old chap?" White Bear asked.

Barlow nodded. "Unless you're scared, hoss."

"Nope. Just wanted to know, that's all, mate."

"That suit you, Black Buffalo?" Barlow asked.

"My medicine is strong," the Flathead said nonchalantly. He sat on his pony proudly, his shield on his left arm, bow in his left hand. His face was freshly painted with jagged yellow lines that resembled lightning. Black and white spots of paint ran in lines up and down his chest and his legs. He wore nothing but a buckskin breechcloth and moccasins.

White Bear, too, was stripped down for battle now, also only wearing a breechcloth—of blanket material—and moccasins. He had tied his shield to loop on the buffalo hide that served as a saddle. He carried his bow and four arrows in his left hand. He was not painted, however.

Barlow looked rather shabby with his worn, torn, bloody cloth shirt and greasy, bloody fringed buckskin pants. His hat was a mess, coated with dirt and sweat, blood and grease. His two saddle pistols were loaded and resting in their holsters. His two belt pistols were in place, and the Colt Paterson was also stuck in his belt. He held his rifle in his right hand, muzzle skyward, the butt resting on his thigh.

"You boys ready?" Barlow asked. When the other two nodded, he said, "Let's go pay them goddamn Blackfeet a little call." He moved forward slowly, then picked up a little speed, until Beelzebub was in a canter. Buffalo trotted alongside him, and White Bear and Black Buffalo were but a pace behind as they headed for the trees. They put a little distance between themselves to present a smaller target.

One arrow, then another, then a fusillade of them came from the trees, but the three riders and the dog were unscathed. It was almost as if they had a protective aura around them.

The riders picked up speed and soon galloped into the thin line of trees. Barlow lowered his rifle and fired at a shadowy figure, knocking the Blackfoot backward and out. He shoved the rifle through a small sling on the front of his saddle and pulled the Colt.

Barlow charged through the trees, firing when he had to, but mainly stayed on the lookout for the two Small Robes. He wanted at least one of them alive and did not want to end up shooting one of them by mistake. A Blackfoot popped up occasionally to try to stop him, but he would shoot the man or ride over him. Buffalo paced Beelzebub, ready to take out any warrior whom Barlow missed.

After a few minutes, Barlow spotted Big Eagle, and he turned the mule after him. Big Eagle saw him coming and jumped on a pony. He raced across the stream, through the trees on the other side and out into the open. Barlow was right behind him, and the big mule quickly cut the distance. He directed Beelzebub up alongside the horse, and then had the mule nudge the Indian pony.

The move knocked the horse's pace off, and it stumbled, throwing Big Eagle.

Barlow pulled to a quick stop a few yards ahead and swung around. Big Eagle was just getting up and began hobbling off across the grassland. It was but a moment before Barlow trotted up alongside him and kicked him in the back, sending him sprawling.

Barlow stopped and dismounted. He looped a rawhide rope around Big Eagle's neck after relieving the Small Robe of his weapons and then tied his hands behind his back with a thong torn from his pants. Barlow mounted the mule and began heading back to where the Blackfeet camp had been, towing an angry, injured Big Eagle behind him.

Buffalo bounded up moments later, sniffing at the Indian, who tried to kick the dog but succeeded only in falling again. Barlow dragged him a little way before stopping long enough for the Small Robe to awkwardly make it to his feet. Then he pressed on.

The Blackfoot sanctuary was almost empty of people. White Bear and Black Buffalo were there, holding Four Dogs, but no living Blackfeet. Several Blackfeet ponies wandered around, seemingly unconcerned about the carnage that had taken place minutes before.

"Sent those boys packin', did you?" Barlow asked.

"Of course, old chap," White Bear said with a harsh grin.

"You two boys gather up all these here Blackfoot ponies that you can. I'll take care of Big Eagle and Four Dogs." He dismounted. "Sit," he ordered Big Eagle. "Buffler, you watch him good." Then he cut some of the rope and tied it around Four Dogs's neck, and then used another fringe from his pants to bind the Small Robe's hands behind his back. He stepped back and waited until White Bear and Black Buffalo had brought in all the ponies they could find.

The two Indians pushed the horses ahead of them, out onto the grassland, heading toward their own herd of animals. Barlow followed closely behind, towing both unhappy Small Robes behind him.

Back with the women and children, White Bear and Black Buffalo ran the Blackfeet ponies in with their own animals.

"All right, folks, we best be on the move," Barlow said, not letting them get comfortable at all. "Those Blackfeet might've run, but I ain't so certain they'll stay away. Besides, we need to find us a place to hole up where we can rest for a spell. And night's comin' on pretty quick."

The others could see no reason to question him. Black Buffalo and White Bear immediately headed out, leading the way as always.

As the women pulled out, herding the horses and mules ahead of them, Barlow moved up to Bull Heart. "You best help the women with those animals, boy," he said. "With all them extra Blackfoot ponies, they got their hands full."

The young Flathead did not like the idea, but he did as he was told.

Barlow—with Buffalo 2 right there with him—brought up the rear, still holding the ropes to the two Small Robes, who were forced to walk. As he rode, he could feel the tiredness settling on him. Now that the battle was over, his adrenaline was dropping, and that always left him tired. Besides, he had not had a decent night's sleep in a couple of days, and he was hungry, which didn't help matters.

They plodded along, Barlow forcing himself to keep awake and to keep a watch on their back trail periodically. He saw no one following them, nor did he get that hunch again. He was relieved at that. He was plain sick of fighting off Indians. He wanted nothing more than a mess of meat, some hot coffee, and a good night's sleep.

More than two hours after they had left, White Bear trotted back and pulled in alongside Barlow. "Black Buffalo says there's a good place to make camp about a mile ahead, old chap. That suit?"

Barlow nodded, wishing the grittiness in his eyes would go away. "You up to makin' meat, hoss?" he asked.

"Of course, old chap." He grinned, but it was weak. He, too, was tired, and it showed on his face. "Especially when there's so much meat about." He pushed ahead and cut two mules out of the herd then pulled away and trotted out across the grass, heading toward a herd of elk less than a hundred yards away. Within ten minutes, he was back, an elk carcass across the back of each of the mules. "This do, mate?" he asked, his grin a little stronger.

"Reckon it does, hoss." Barlow managed a small grin himself.

Fifteen minutes later, they pulled to a halt along the same stream that the Blackfeet had used. A deep thicket of trees would offer plenty of protection as well as forage and wood. The whole group wearily set about their tasks in making camp.

Barlow tied his two prisoners to a tree, then went to help unload their supplies. A few of the women were gathering firewood and water, while the others set to butchering the elk White Bear had brought in. Black Buffalo—in an unusual action for him—and White Bear took care of the pack animals, hobbling them and allowing them to graze. The four men also tended to their riding mounts. Finally the meat was cooked and the coffee was ready. They all sat, the men, plus Raven Moon, Far Thunder, and Yellow Leaf at one fire, the other women and children at another. They ate quietly, seeing no need to talk just yet.

"Give food!" Big Eagle shouted. "Give food!"

"Get knotted, you bloody stupid bastard," White Bear snapped back at them.

"Want food!" Four Dogs threw in.

"Shut that flappin' hole of yours, boy," Barlow growled.

"Food!" Four Dogs demanded. "Give food now!"

With a sigh, Barlow rose, went to the packs of supplies, where he cut off a couple of strips of buckskin. Then he went to the two captives, who were continuing to shout, and gagged them. They still made noise, but it was muffled, and they soon even gave that up.

After polishing off several servings of hot, juicy elk meat, Barlow lit his pipe. He leaned back with a mug of coffee and stretched out his legs. He closed his eyes as he puffed on the pipe. It had been a hell of a couple of days, he thought. But tomorrow they should reach Black Buffalo's village and be shed of the Flatheads. Then he could get back to looking for Anna. Of course, first he had to question the Small Robes. It was something he did not look forward to because of what he would likely have to do. On the other hand, he hoped it would get him some real information on where Anna was. That made facing whatever he had to do a little easier to take.

"What're you going to do about those two bloody buggers we captured, old chap?" White Bear asked, breaking Barlow from his reverie.

"Gonna have a nice long chat with 'em," Barlow said grimly. "I still think they lied to us before when they talked about Anna and them other young'uns. In fact, seein' as how they threw in with the other Blackfeet, I'm certain they lied to us. And I aim to get 'em to speak true."

"You do it now?" Bull Heart asked. He sounded almost eager.

"Nope," Barlow said. "This chil' needs some robe time. 'Sides, lettin' 'em sit and stew all night might do wonders for their humors. Might even make 'em more willin' to talk come mornin'."

"Smart," Black Buffalo said with a harsh grin.

Barlow nodded. A few minutes later, he knocked the ashes from his pipe and slurped down the rest of his coffee. "As I said, this ol' chil' needs some robe time." He rose and, accompanied by Raven Moon, who left Yellow Leaf with the other women, went off to the side a little way and spread out his otter-skin sleeping robe. It was still light, though the day was fading fast.

Barlow winced as he pulled off his shirt. Raven Moon looked at him in surprise. "One of those damned Blackfeet whacked me good with a war club," he said, turning so she could see his back.

Raven Moon gasped at the purplish-yellow bruise that marred his powerful upper shoulder area on the right side. She touched it gently. "It look bad," she said.

"I'll survive," he said. He turned and grinned as he took her in his arms. "I jist might have to be careful in our doin's tonight."

"We'll find a way that won't hurt," Raven Moon promised. She smiled, then she pulled his head down to kiss him, which she did with considerable ardor. It had the effect on him that she desired, too.

He stepped back so he could drop his belt and pants. She, in turn, slipped out of her plain buckskin dress. After another hot kiss, Barlow eased Raven Moon down onto the sleeping robe and stretched out beside her. His hands played her love organ with all the expertise and interest he had in him, and she soon began squirming and moaning in appreciation of his efforts.

As she built to a climax, Barlow increased his efforts, and soon she was shuddering in the throes of passion. When she relaxed minutely, Barlow began his ministrations again, bringing her higher and higher. When this climax burst through her, she pulled his face down and kissed him hard.

Barlow finally pulled away and gently rolled Raven Moon over on her stomach and lifted her buttocks. He slid around until he was behind her and between her legs. He entered her easily from behind, slowly inserting himself and reveling in the pleasures her womanhood endowed on him. She moaned softly and wriggled her rear end against him, letting him know that she, too, was enjoying it immensely.

He moved out almost all the way, then sank back in. He slowly repeated his movements over and over, and then increased his pace. The tiredness sloughed off him as the ecstasy began building in his groin. He soon softly growled his release, the harsh sounds mingling with Raven Moon's higher-pitched squeals of delight.

Finally, Barlow slumped to the side, overcome with pleasure. As he fought to regain his breath, the exhaustion swept over him again. He kissed Raven Moon lightly and immediately fell asleep.

He felt considerably better in the morning when he awoke, even though he almost immediately remembered that he was going to question Big Eagle and Four Dogs soon. But that didn't matter. He was refreshed and fully prepared to do what was needed to help find Anna.

He rose and pulled on his clothes, moving a little gingerly, as his back still hurt considerably. Raven Moon was not there, and he figured she was already at the fire.

He found her there, cooking meat. White Bear was also there, with Far Thunder. Black Buffalo and Bull Heart arrived moments later.

Raven Moon greeted Barlow with a kiss, then made him sit as she served him his meal.

19

BARLOW ATE BREAKFAST rather swiftly. Now that he had made up his mind on what he had to do, he was eager to get it over with. Besides, he wanted to get what information he could so that he could get the Flatheads back to their village and get back on the trail after Anna.

On the other hand, he was not in such a great hurry. And, since he was done earlier than everyone else, he lit his pipe and tried to relax a little. The others soon finished and either sat sipping coffee or puffing on pipes.

Barlow finally knocked the ashes from his pipe and stood. Without a word, he headed for the two Small Robes. The other men followed closely, silently. They were still a grim group. They stopped and squatted in a semicircle in front of the two Small Robe Blackfeet. Barlow tore the gags off the two captives.

"Black Buffalo, translate for me, like you did last time," Barlow said harshly. "Make sure these boys know exactly what I'm sayin' to 'em."

Black Buffalo nodded.

Barlow glared at Four Dogs. "You lied to me, hoss,"

he said, giving Black Buffalo a moment to translate. "It don't shine with me to be lied to." He didn't care that Black Buffalo wouldn't be able to translate his words perfectly, just as long as the Small Robes understood his meaning. "Now, I want to know what happened to my little Anna—where she is and who has her."

"I told you, she was taken north, into the land of the Hudson's Bay people," Four Dogs said through Black Buffalo.

"That's a goddamn lie, boy, and I know it as well as you do. Now speak true."

"I speak with straight tongue."

Barlow bit back the fury that enveloped him and forced himself to remain calm. "You best realize, hoss," he said tightly, "that I will do anythin' to find my Anna, includin' tearin' you limb from limb." He paused while the Flathead leader translated. "Now I know you're a brave warrior," he continued, "and ain't afraid to go under. Mayhap ain't even afraid of bein' tortured. But, I reckon you ain't quite so brave about facing the Hereafter as less than a whole man."

Barlow paused to let Black Buffalo translate again, and to give Four Dogs a few moments for that information to sink in.

"I am right ready to put you under, and then butcher you to make sure you never make it to the Happy Huntin' Ground as a real man. First, I'll raise your hair, boy, so your spirit'll never be free. I'll carve out your heart so's you have no bravery against your enemies in the Hereafter. I'll crack your leg and arm bones, so you can't defend yourself or your family there. And I'll tear out your eyes so you can't see the enemy and cut out your tongue so you can't talk with your ancestors. I'll smash out your teeth so that you cannot enjoy the buffler that are so plentiful in the afterlife."

Barlow paused again, giving Four Dogs time to digest all that. Then he added, "You'll be a ragged, poor excuse for a warrior and a man, a shame to your people and to your ancestors. You'll be no good for anythin'."

Fear suddenly appeared in Four Dogs's dark eyes. He was not certain this white man was wild enough to do all he had said he would, but he couldn't be sure that he wasn't, either. He had seen some of these white men do such things before.

" 'Course, you tell me the truth, and mayhap you'll die a warrior's death," Barlow went on. "And I'll let you go to the Spirit Land in one piece. I'll do the same for your pal over there." He nodded at Big Eagle. "So, what's it gonna be, hoss?"

Big Eagle suddenly began speaking to Four Dogs in his own language, the words tumbling over one another.

"What the hell's he sayin', Black Buffalo?" Barlow asked in annoyance.

"He's telling Four Dogs to talk."

Barlow nodded. "So, how about it, hoss?" Barlow asked Four Dogs when Big Eagle had finished talking.

"I talk," Four Dogs said in heavily accented English after a considerable amount of thought. "I speak true."

Barlow nodded. "So, out with it, hoss."

"After you and the Shoshoni drive off the Blackfeet," Four Bears answered through Black Buffalo, "they took the children to their village. They keep the children over the winter. When spring come, a group of Blackfeet went south with the children. They planned to trade them to the Utes for horses and weapons."

"What in hell would the Utes want with a bunch of captured young'uns?" Barlow asked.

"The Utes capture—or sometimes buy—children from other tribes whenever and however they can. They trade 'em to the white-eyes chief at a trading post in Ute country. That trader sends them to Taos and Santa Fe, where the Mexicans buy 'em for slaves."

Barlow sat there as the horror of Anna's situation washed over him. He could not believe that such a thing went on, but he could see no reason for the Small Robe to lie to him about this. Not this time. Slowly he realized that it was all too plausible. All of it. Indians had been enslaving captives for as long as forever, if the stories were to be believed. It was not all that unthinkable that Mexicans would buy Indian children for slaves.

But to think that Anna would be among them was almost too much to bear. It sent a shiver of disgust and worry through him. "Where is this tradin' post?" he demanded, his voice stern and unforgiving.

"Don't know," Four Dogs said through Black Buffalo.

"All we know," Big Eagle hastily interjected when he saw the anger flare in Barlow's eyes, "is that it is in Ute country." He spoke slowly in his own language, giving Black Buffalo time to translate for him, too. "We think a white-eyed named Robidoux is the chief there."

"One of the Robidoux brothers, I'd say, mate," White Bear said evenly.

Barlow nodded tightly. "I've heard of them. Can't say as I know them, but I've heard the name more'n once in my mountain days." He let the anger and disgust—and a pinch of despair—simmer inside him for some minutes, until it was almost at a boil.

Barlow glanced at White Bear, who stared blankly back at him. The Shoshoni knew what Barlow was thinking. Barlow wanted nothing more than to leave immediately and go after Anna.

The former mountain man was torn. He did want to leave this moment and head for Ute country. But he had made a promise to Black Buffalo and the others, and at this point, so close to the Flathead village, he could not go back on his word.

"You got anything else to tell me, hoss?" he asked harshly, looking from Four Dogs to Big Eagle as Black Buffalo translated.

Both warriors shook their heads. Four Dogs looked almost defiant, but fear shone large in Big Eagle's eyes.

Barlow nodded, wondering what to do now. He could not, in good conscience, let the two live. But he was not so hard-hearted as to want to just kill them in cold blood like this.

"Go and start loadin' the supplies, old chap," White Bear said quietly. "We'll take care of things here."

Barlow looked at him, not quite comprehending. Then he turned his sights on Black Buffalo. The Flathead nodded, and realization began to spread through Barlow. "You certain?" he asked, looking from Black Buffalo to White Bear.

Both nodded.

"This really ain't your doin's, boys," Barlow offered as a mild protest.

"You wrong," Black Buffalo said. "These two betrayed my people, brought the Blackfeet down on us." The Flathead's anger was rising now, too. "Because of them, we all almost die. Maybe they brought the Blackfeet against us before, too. Before you and White Bear come along to help. If so, they killed my son and others of the People."

"And they tried bloody hard to kill me, too, old chap," White Bear added. "As you're so fond of saying, mate, that doesn't shine with this old chap."

Barlow didn't need to give it much consideration. White Bear and Black Buffalo had as much reason to hate the two Small Robes as he did, maybe more. After all, as far as he knew, the two Small Robes had really not had anything to do with Anna's disappearance in the first place, or with her being taken to Ute country. All they had done was lie to him about what had happened to her, which, if they had not finally spoken the truth, would have caused him months more of fruitless searching. It was reason enough to hate them and want them dead, but White Bear and Black Buffalo had at least as much reason to want to kill them.

"Might be that I'll jist stick around," Barlow finally said.

"It will not be pretty, old chap," White Bear said flatly.

Barlow nodded, understanding. He rose and turned, but spun back when Four Dogs said in his heavily accented English, "You say we die like warriors. Go to Spirit World good." He sounded worried.

"What I said, hoss, was that I wouldn't do nothin' to prevent you from enterin' the afterlife in one piece. I didn't never say that someone else wouldn't do so." He spun on his heel and stalked away, Buffalo at his side, to the sound of Four Dogs and Big Eagle beginning to sing their death songs, the strains of the odd sounds flitting up through the trees.

Barlow busied himself with loading supplies—there were not that many left at this point—and tried to ignore the sounds from where White Bear and the two Flathead warriors were dispatching Four Dogs and Big Eagle. Not that it was noisy. The two Small Robes continued singing their death songs, though the voices grew faint after a few minutes and continued to fade until they were silenced. Barlow tried not to think of what was being done to the two enemies now. Not that he had much compassion for them—as far as he was concerned, they deserved whatever was being done to them—but he had always found such excesses distasteful, no matter who was performing them.

He was finished loading the meager supplies on a couple of mules and just beginning to saddle Beelzebub when White Bear, Black Buffalo, and Bull Heart approached. The two Flatheads just nodded at him and kept walking to get their ponies.

White Bear stopped next to Barlow. "They died well, old chap," he said evenly. "But they will be no bloody danger to us—or anyone else—in the Spirit World."

"It was goddamn necessary," Barlow said flatly.

White Bear nodded. He hesitated, but then spoke quietly, "Don't think too poorly of me, old chap. I might've had a white man's education and was raised for some time in an English home, but deep down, I'm Shoshoni. And I believe in my people's ways. What we did to Four Dogs and Big Eagle made perfect sense in our lights, my friend. Reasons that come from the Great Spirit and must be obeyed."

Barlow stared at White Bear for a few moments, then nodded. "You're right, hoss," he said. "It ain't right for me to judge your ways jist 'cause they're different than mine." He smiled grimly. "And I reckon your ways was right in these doin's."

White Bear nodded.

"You best git ready, hoss," Barlow said, clapping White Bear on the shoulder. "I aim to git on the trail here right quick. We should be able to git to White Bear's village well before dark. I don't want to waste no more time. Anna's waitin' for me to come git her, and I reckon we're gonna find her this time."

White Bear nodded again. "I'll be ready when you are, mate." He hurried off.

Within half an hour they pulled out, forming the same column as before. But there was a difference now—

there was an excitement among the Flatheads that was almost palpable. They knew they were close to home and were happy about it. The exhilaration extended to Barlow and White Bear, though not as strongly. Still, both would be glad when their task was over and they could get back to the real business at hand.

The anticipation increased shortly after the sun reached its high point for the day, and by midafternoon the village they sought was in sight. A group of warriors raced out and with great glee greeted their weary friends, who had been gone so long.

Barlow and White Bear were escorted into the village as heroes, and the head chief, Strong Elk, greeted them warmly. The old chief declared that a feast in honor of the two visitors was in order. White Bear and Barlow sat talking with Strong Elk for a while.

Black Buffalo soon came and got Barlow and White Bear. The three, with Bull Heart, Raven Moon, Far Thunder, and several others rode a mile or so off. There, in stark loneliness, rested Father Sylvestre Lambert on a Flathead funeral scaffold. There was no burial ground nearby, and the Flatheads were reluctant to lay the priest to rest in one of their cemeteries anyway. The corpse was clad in a clean cassock—the Flatheads had found it in his meager bag of personal items—and had his Rosary beads and large cross resting on his chest.

"Is good?" Black Buffalo asked.

Barlow nodded. "He weren't much of a man by my lights, all in all," he said. "But he acquitted himself well at the end, and for that he deserves to go to the Spirit World and live in peace."

They all stood in silence for a few minutes, none of them being given much to praying, but wanting to honor a man who had died to save another. Then they quietly rode back to the village.

Raven Moon and Far Thunder took Barlow and White Bear away to their lodges, where the women gratefully thanked the two men quite well for their help in getting them and all the others home safe.

Knowing it was too late in the day to leave anyway, Barlow could not see arguing with the thanks he received from Raven Moon. Nor could he object to the celebration that began just as night started to fall.

20

BARLOW AND RAVEN Moon slipped away from the feasting and dancing fairly soon after it all began. They stayed long enough for Barlow to regale the Flatheads with some of his deeds and to fill his belly. But by then he just wanted to be alone with Raven Moon. She was of like mind.

With Raven Moon's enthusiasm and Barlow's strong desire, it was a long though highly enjoyable night. They finally fell asleep in each other's arms, glad to be there and happy to have made it to the village at long last. For Barlow, there was also the joy of knowing that he would soon be out looking for Anna again. He would hate to leave Raven Moon, but it would have to be done. He had come to enjoy her more than anyone he had met since his Sarah had died, but he could not bring her along, and he was not about to forgo his search for Anna, for Raven Moon or anyone. But he was glad that his last few hours with the Flathead woman were so pleasant. It would give him good memories to carry with him on the long, hard trail.

He didn't get much sleep, but he still felt pretty good in the morning, especially after he and Raven Moon made love one more time. His back still hurt, but he mostly ignored it. She then brought him coffee and freshly roasted meat. When he had finished eating, he leisurely rose and dressed. Then he kissed Raven Moon passionately just before stepping outside the lodge.

"You will come back?" Raven Moon asked in a tentative voice when they were outside.

"Reckon that wouldn't put me out none," Barlow allowed. "But I got to find my Anna first, and that may take some doin's."

"I'd like you to come back," Raven Moon said shyly.

"And I'd like to come back, Raven Moon. You're a fine woman. A man couldn't ask for none better."

"Ready to go, old chap?" White Bear asked, walking up with Far Thunder.

"Reckon so," Barlow said tentatively, looking around. "Soon's Buffler shows up."

"Looks like we're not the only ones enjoying carnal pleasures, mate," White Bear said with a laugh.

"I reckon that's what he's up to," Barlow agreed, also laughing. "But he best finish up his business mighty goddamn soon."

"Strong Elk said we can have whatever supplies they got that we're short of, old chap," White Bear said. "Black Buffalo says all the ponies we took from the bloody Blackfeet are ours."

"We don't need 'em," Barlow allowed. "Let the Flatheads have 'em all. As payment for the supplies. Maybe we can git 'em back one day when we have more need for 'em. We'll jist take our mules, and your pony, of course."

White Bear nodded. "I'll go tell Strong Elk. And start gathering up our bloody supplies."

"I'll be along directly to help load them mules," Barlow said as White Bear and Far Thunder strolled off. Barlow and Raven Moon went back inside the lodge and had more coffee and then headed outside again. Buffalo 2 was there, lying just outside the lodge. He rose, his tail wagging, when Barlow spotted him. The two people and the dog headed off toward the Flathead herds and began culling out their animals. While they were doing so, White Bear strolled by and told Barlow where he would be with the supplies, and then he left.

With the animals roped together, Barlow and Raven Moon headed to where White Bear was waiting. The two men swiftly loaded what supplies they had—mostly coffee, some tea, sugar, salt, a bit of flour, and a supply of pemmican and jerky. It did not take long. Then Barlow saddled Beelzebub, and White Bear prepared his pony.

Each man kissed his woman good-bye and then mounted his animal. They nodded to the women and rode slowly out of the village, waving to some of the people.

Just at the edge of the village, Black Buffalo and Bull Heart were waiting. Barlow and White Bear stopped. "May the Great Spirit be with you in your search," Black Buffalo said seriously. "And may your medicine be strong."

"Thank you, Black Buffalo," Barlow responded in kind. "I reckon I can use all the help I can get." He looked at Bull Heart. "You listen to your elders, boy," he said, a faint smile tugging at his lips. "You do that, and you jist might live long enough to git yourself a woman."

Bull Heart nodded.

Barlow and White Bear pulled out then, not looking back. Half a mile out of the village, they picked up the pace. With just the two of them and the dog they could move at a good clip. They headed south, not really sure where they were going, only that they were looking for a trading post run by someone named Robidoux in Ute country.

On the long ride, monotony hanging heavy on him, Barlow began to wonder if the two Small Robes had lied to him a second time despite his threats. The thought plagued him, sparking a deep concern that he would never find the trading post, let along his daughter. It ate at him, making him cross and short tempered.

White Bear let him be, riding silently along with his own thoughts, most of which centered on returning home someday. He was not at all sorry that he had joined Barlow on this quest, but there were times when he missed the companionship of his own people. Around the camp, he was quiet, too, talking only when necessary or when his friend had those infrequent times when he felt like some conversation.

Even with pushing their pace, it took them almost three weeks just to get to Ute country. Then they started hunting for Robidoux's fort. Being an unknown—to the Utes—white man riding with a Shoshoni, it was difficult to find any of those Indians willing to talk to them, but the two persevered, until finally they found a small hunting party of Utes who weren't all that unfriendly. Barlow offered them some salt—always a precious commodity out here—and some sugar, which many Indians loved, in exchange for some information.

"You must go to Uncompahgre country," one of the Utes said in heavily accented English.

"Where the hell is that?" Barlow asked.

"Southwest. Three days' ride. Maybe four. Follow Gunnison River," he pointed south, "half day ride. Fort where Uncompahgre River flows into Gunnison River. You find, no trouble."

Barlow wasn't sure whether to believe him or not, but he really had no choice. "You know this Robidoux feller?" he asked.

"Robidoux good man."

Barlow nodded. He and White Bear rose, mounted their animals, and rode out. Barlow did not like nor trust these Utes, though he hoped they had spoken the truth. That night, the two travelers made a small camp along what they figured was the Gunnison River. The next morning, they began following it. And two days after that, they pulled to a stop, Barlow cursing a blue streak. They had come to a deep, dark canyon where the river boiled through, offering no way to pass. In anger and disappointment, they turned around, rode almost a full day back the way they had come, and then turned south, hoping to skirt the forbidding canyon.

They did so, but it took them two days longer than they had planned on, and when they picked up another river, they were not sure it was the right one. Following it north, they soon decided that it was the Uncompahgre, and they picked up speed again, figuring they were close to the fort.

Late the next morning, they spotted the small, log trading post and soon rode inside it. As they did, snow began falling again—it had done so most of the past three days, and the temperature dropped. It was October now, and they were not surprised by the snow, though Barlow chafed in knowing that the heart of winter weather would sweep over the mountains very soon, meaning his time was growing short.

A tall, thin, distinguished looking man stepped out of one of the log buildings. "Welcome," he said. *"Bonjour. Hola."* He wore fine, almost dandified clothes, but he still carried the air of a man used to the wilderness and its hardships.

Barlow and White Bear stopped their animals right in front of the man. "You Robidoux?"

"*Oui*. Yes I am." He had a slight French accent. "Antoine Robidoux at your service, monsieurs." He bowed slightly. "And you are?" He still seemed pleasant, but a hard look had suddenly appeared in his eyes.

"Name's Will Barlow." He dismounted and shook hands. "My friend there is White Bear."

Robidoux nodded at the Shoshoni. "You monsieurs have come far?" he asked.

"Plenty far," Barlow responded, not trying to hide his sarcasm.

"Some Utes told me zere was a white man and an Indian—possibly Shoshoni—looking for zis fort. Now zat you 'ave found it, and *moi*, what can I do for you?"

"I'm lookin' for my daughter," Barlow said. "Young gal. She's mayhap four or five now."

"Why would you think she was 'ere?" Robidoux asked, somewhat surprised.

"From what I been told, hoss, you buy Injin children—captives—from the Utes and send 'em down to Santa Fe to be sold to the goddamn Mexicans as slaves." Rage sprang up in his heart.

Robidoux looked as if he had been slapped, but he managed to calm his rising anger. As slightly built as he was, he did not want to tangle with a man as wide and strong as Barlow obviously was, despite his years in the mountains. "Zis is not ze kind of thing to be discussed out 'ere in ze open. Come to my quarters, monsieurs. We will 'ave meat and some whiskey to take ze chill off your bones."

Barlow hesitated only a moment before nodding.

"One moment, monsieurs," Robidoux said. He leaned

back inside the building and spoke for a few moments in fluent Spanish. Two young men, Mexicans by the look of them, came out. "Zese boys will take care of your animals, monsieurs. Zey will be safe."

Barlow nodded again, and White Bear dismounted. With the former carrying his rifle, and the latter his bow, the two, accompanied by Buffalo 2, followed Robidoux diagonally across the small plaza and into a room.

"Sit, monsieurs," Barlow said, pointing to several wooden chairs grouped around a small wooden table. As they did, the trader turned to the Ute woman standing by the fire. He spoke to her in what Barlow assumed was her language, then he took a seat at the table. Within moments, the woman had placed tin plates and cups before each of the men, then made another trip with a platter of roasted buffalo meat and once more with a clay jug of whiskey.

Robidoux poured them each a full serving of whiskey, and the men drank a healthy mouthful. The heat of the whiskey settled in their stomachs, producing a warm glow. Outside, the wind picked up strongly.

"Now, monsieur," Robidoux asked, reaching for a hunk of meat with his belt knife, "what is zis about your daughter?"

Barlow took a deep breath and another large slug of whiskey, then explained about how Anna was originally taken, how she came to be in White Bear's possession for a while, and her loss to Bob Carruthers and the Blackfeet.

"We got a couple of Small Robe Blackfeet to tell us that the other Blackfeet bands had taken Anna—and a passel of other young'uns—down this way and traded 'em off to the Utes, who were expected to bring 'em here so they could be took down to Santa Fe or Taos and sold as slaves." The rage was back at the very thought that this trader had had a hand in such an appalling activity.

Robidoux could plainly read Barlow's mood. "I understand your anger at me, monsieur," he said. "But you must understand zat ze children ze Utes bring 'ere are Indian children. Ze Mexicans 'ave been enslaving Indians forever, I suppose. I am a friend of ze Utes, who 'ave been good to me, and zis is a way of 'elping my friends weaken zeir enemies."

Barlow nodded and shrugged, not really caring about Robidoux's reasoning. To him it was a heinous thing that Robidoux was doing, but, really, all he wanted right now was to find Anna.

"I did not really see any of ze children," Robidoux continued when Barlow said nothing. "So I don't know if your daughter was among zem, but if ze Blackfeet were telling ze truth, then I suppose she was."

"You didn't see 'em?" Barlow demanded angrily.

"*Non.* I let one of my clerks 'andle it zis time. I was occupied with other things."

"You should've paid more attention, hoss," Barlow growled.

"Perhaps. I will say, monsieur, zat if I 'ad realized one of zem was a white—or partially white—girl, I would not 'ave allowed 'er to leave 'ere."

"How long they been gone?"

"Many weeks. Since about mid-summer."

Barlow nodded, despair beginning to mingle with his rage. He knew now that she would already be enslaved in some Mexican household. He had always had the hope—though deep in his heart he knew it was forlorn—that he would get here and find out Anna had just been taken and that he could catch her on the trail before she got to the Mexican cities. But that hope was now dashed.

Barlow ate some meat and sipped at the whiskey just

to have something to do. Without it, he might have killed Robidoux, even though he knew that would do him absolutely no good. So he ate and drank, waiting for the anger to subside and the despair to reach its limit before it, too, began to ebb.

"I am sorry, monsieur," Robidoux said, apparently meaning it. "I wish zere was something I could do."

"I don't reckon you know exactly where she was taken? Or if the folks who brought her down there are around and might know who bought her?" Barlow asked, not expecting a positive answer.

"*Non*, monsieur. Zey were to go to Taos first, and zen on to Santa Fe. Zey will not return until ze spring." He shrugged, helpless to provide any assistance.

Barlow ate some more, polished off the mug of whiskey, and stood. "Well, thank you, Mister Robidoux," he said. "I appreciate your hospitality, but I best be on my way." He looked at White Bear. "You can stay here, hoss, if you're of a mind to—and if Mister Robidoux will have you."

"Zere is room for you both, monsieur," Robidoux said. "I think it is foolish of you to consider leaving now."

"Obliged, Mister Robidoux," Barlow said. "But I got to find Anna."

"And I'm going with him, old chap," White Bear said, standing. He grabbed a last piece of meat to take with him.

Barlow and White Bear stepped outside and were slammed hard by the howling wind. It was snowing harder than Barlow had ever seen, and the temperature had plummeted. As used to harsh winters as he and White Bear were, they would not make it a mile in such a storm. It was likely that they would die long before reaching Taos.

Barlow stood there a few moments, dreaming once again of the day he would find Anna. In the teeth of the raging storm, he bowed his head, unaware that White Bear had gone back inside and that Buffalo was looking strangely at him. "Don't you worry, little girl," he said softly, but with fierce determination, "I aim to follow you until the end of my life, if that's what it takes, to bring you home."

With the despair threatening to swallow him again, Barlow turned and went back inside the cabin, a worried Buffalo at his side.

LONGARM

Explore the exciting Old West with one of the men who made it wild!